Praise for *Scars Of Shadow* and Alyssa Askani

"Fans of true dark fantasy, Dark Souls games, Lords of the Fallen and who enjoy complex and interesting characters will thoroughly appreciate this book."

—A.J. Forster, author of *The Voice of the World*

"It's like *The Dark Crystal* if it was directed by Sam Raimi."

—Mike Jack Stoumbos, author of *This Fine Crew*

"This tale was a visit to the darker side of fantasy with rich description, deep worldbuilding, and a cursed witch who embodies the true nature of a hero… Here is an inspiring portrayal of humanity's fiercest trait: Courage when all seems lost."

—Jen Bair, author of *One Good Eye*

Tales of the Night Lands

ALYSSA ASKANI

CONTENTS

WELCOME TO THE NIGHT LANDS

This is my most brutal setting. If you're after some existential dread, you'll find it the longer you look at the foundational elements that makes this world work.

If you're craving adventure and excitement, you'll get it, but there are prices to be paid. Some of those costs burrow holes in one's identity. Maybe even their soul.

This is not a friendly place.

This is the kind of world you visit when you need to see the horrors others can inflict. This is where you go when you want to find your way out the most oppressive struggles.

There are stories sweeping between the text you'll soon read. Heroes and villains assembling to confront their world. Some are overt and rule the narrative. Others are hiding from Helio-Asura as much as they're hiding from me.

Join me now. Explore what it means to not only survive in a cruel world, but to thrive in spite of it.

—Alyssa Askani

HOPE OF THE HATCHLING

I am the golden coil
Bound by a heedless call
No one to speak of
No soul to know

The cry of my birth
beckoned true
Set me loose
Link to you

When do you come?
Wings lay empty
Freedom denied
The longer I wait.

HUNTING FOR SHABRA-LAI

As rain swept through the stone streets, tall lanterns marked a path through the rare darkness. With so many clouds shading the eternal sun from view, the heat subsided, and the air became pleasant. Sounds of trickling water filled every puddle. A low rumble of thunder moaned in the distance.

On top of the central beacon tower, a gem glowed through the torrential rain. Ephrem admired a line in the left side of the gem as his mantorse ambled down the main street. He found a corral lit by a nearby alehouse.

Ephrem pulled his mantorse close to the corral, lashing the long arthropod where it couldn't dart away. He hoped the lightning would stay away. The animal rode well, and Ephrem didn't want it to turn timid. A mantorse was no dragon, but not everyone had connections to merchant routes, military squadrons, or religious pilgrimages.

He brushed his hand along the mantorse's spine before petting the sides of its face. Ephrem noticed the flexing of his steed's mandibles, along with the way the creature looked at him with its compound eyes. From one of the saddlebags, Ephrem pulled out a pouch full of a dark mush filled with worms. The mantorse ate for a minute before Ephrem put the pouch away and walked to the alehouse.

Easing a leather tarp away from the entrance, Ephrem pushed through the double doors of the ale house. Aged grooves scratched the doors. Hooting laughter of an excited a drunken crowd.

A variety of people sat at round tables throughout the ale hall, most in groups of two or three. Soldiers in cracked ceramic armor eclipsed one table. A pair of wealthy women draped in jewels and colorful layers of dragon weave sat off to the side. Several merchants filled the rest of the space, keeping their satchels close to their hands. A few scattered women wore slight skirts and even more slight tops. A musician pushed the floor pedals at the base of a long tube, forcing a lively sound from his stomp flute. Ephrem tossed a coin into the wood tray on the musician's table. The musician nodded.

From the ale counter, a scrawny man with a scraggly beard barked. "You there. What god you pray to?" The crowd quieted a little.

Ephrem took off a wide-brimmed hat, letting his blond braid fall down his left side. Lightly shaking his head, he said, "I pray to no god."

The bearded man lifted a rounded ceramic blade, which had a dim glow. "Who'd your parents pray to? And don't say no one or I'll cut you right out that door."

"Zoya."

The bearded man dropped his knife on the counter. "Zoya? I haven't seen a Zoyan in thirty seasons."

"Forty-three seasons for me," Ephrem said. He stepped further into the ale house, shaking the rain off his tunic. "My parents died in an Asurian raid." Ephrem threw another coin to the musician. A lively rhythm filled the ale house once more.

"Damned Asurians." Most of the crowd kept talking. The bearded man slammed a mug of ale on the counter. "Wish they'd kill themselves and leave the rest of us in peace."

"I'll drink to that."

Both men raised their mugs and drank, taking in far more than a simple swallow. As Ephrem put his mug back on the counter, he wiped a bit of foam from his upper lip. "Fine ale, sir, fine indeed."

"Thank you," the bearded man said. "It's Rex, not sir."

"Ephrem. And it's a fine ale." He meant it, not just because he hadn't tasted an ale in ages, but because he'd traveled for so long, he needed to taste something other than the water from his skins.

"So," Rex said, leaning close. "What brings you here, Ephrem? I don't think you came to hear me tell how my momma burned in a Ka-whe temple."

For a moment, Ephrem wondered if the Asurians had killed Rex's mother. It didn't seem worth digging up, since the two had just met. "Commerce. I have a map that's worth a great deal."

Rex refilled his mug. "Lots of people have maps in these parts. What would make yours special?"

"Honestly?" Ephrem weighed his decision for a moment, but he knew he couldn't keep the map's details and nature secret, not if he meant to profit from them. He drank the rest of his ale, then slid the empty mug toward Rex. "Fill me up again and I'll tell you about it."

In moments, Rex poured another round of ale, not just for Ephrem, but for himself as well. As he put the mugs on the counter, he said, "You've got my curiosity. Just don't let me down with some scam."

"I don't intend to." Ephrem drew a rolled sheet of leather from his coat and put it on the table next to the two mugs. He unwound the waxed twine from both ends, then picked up the fresh mug of ale. "Take a look."

Rex looked at Ephrem for a moment, then started unrolling the leather sheet. Inside, a smaller sheet of leather lay over a long piece of parchment with five scattered circles marked on it, along with a small black dot close to the upper edge. After a moment of looking at the parchment, Rex shook his head. "This is nothing."

"That's the point. It's not supposed to look like anything. If it looks harmless, no one will think anything of it. Only when you go a step further do you find more." Ephrem reached into his jacket and took out a thick piece of glass embedded with a trio of crystals. "Look through this."

The disappointment took over Rex's face, his expression having shifted to something more pitying than anything else. He looked through the glass. Ephrem recalled the image through the glass. A set of hazy numbered lines connected every circle in a cryptic sequence.

Rex gingerly lowered the glass onto the parchment. He sat back, silenced by a thousand thoughts.

Ephrem let Rex stew in a moment of quiet. With any luck, there would be explanation and negotiation. "What did you see?"

"Lines and numbers that weren't there before."

"Anything else?"

"No." Rex reached for the thick glass, but Ephrem put his hand over it.

"Those numbers are measurements," Ephrem said. "Each circle represents a beacon tower. Help someone find their destination if they're out in a storm."

"It's useless in the sun."

Ephrem pointed up at the ceiling. "When storms come, our eternal sun is a little harder to find."

"Sure."

"Beacon towers are common enough, especially since they're often the only respite during bad weather. These beacons, however, are all marked with a single black line running over the top of the crystal. Now." Ephrem took his hand off the glass. "Look again."

Rex picked up the glass and looked at the circles. "There's a line in each one."

"That says how those lines are positioned. If we went outside and looked at the beacon tower, we'd see such a line. There's something else as well." He pointed at a blank spot well away from the circles.

Rex looked closer for a moment, then put down the glass and scratched his beard. "Shabra-Lai?"

Ephrem nodded.

After taking a long drink of ale, Rex asked, "This is a map to get to Shabra-Lai?"

"Yes."

"Why haven't you used it? You could get off the ground. Even the poor people in Shabra-Lai live like kings. They have all the water they could drink, live above the worst of the weather, and they have dragons—and no Asurians."

"For now," a female voice said.

Ephrem turned around and saw a woman standing next to him. She'd made no sound as she approached. Both her skin and hair were the shade of roasted almonds, ensuring the sun would never wound her. Surprising sweetness filled her breath, matching the slight fragrance of her skin. She wore a crimson top over her breasts and tapped the bit of gold in her navel.

The woman leaned close and said, "It's only a matter of time until an Asurian gets up there and enlightens the floating city. Anyone who makes that happen would be very wealthy. Imperia Kagatsu has offered a dragon's load of gold to anyone who can tell her where Shabra-Lai is."

Ephrem put the smaller sheet of leather over the parchment. "It's the only major power that's in her way."

"Them and the Zolas Republic," Rex said.

"They don't have dragons." Ephrem rolled up the map and put the seeing glass in his pocket.

"What if I offered to make you an introduction?" the woman asked. "You wouldn't even have to go to an Asurian city. I could arrange a meeting wherever you prefer. They'll make you a handsome offer. I'll pay you just to hear them out."

Ephrem turned toward the woman. She had the kind of lovely face that had been trained to craft honeyed temptations. Even if she wanted an honest transaction, she was far too dangerous.

So Ephrem drew a knife from his sleeve and buried it in her throat.

She gurgled and fell limp.

As he pulled his knife free, Ephrem found himself the focus of all the attention in the alehouse. The women in slight clothes leaned up from their guests. Music stopped streaming from the stomp flute. Ephrem took another coin from his pocket and tossed it to the musician. He returned to his drink, setting his knife beside Rex's. "As I was saying, there are lines on the beacon crystals and the map. But without the last secret, it can't be used to find Shabra-Lai."

"There's more?" Rex glanced at the leather roll containing the map. "I didn't see anything else."

"You saw everything. This isn't something that you can read." Ephrem finished bundling the map back together. "The beacon crystals are arrows. You have to find a way to pick out which way they're pointing."

Satisfied with his demonstration, Ephrem caressed the edges of the map. He exhaled, satisfied that everyone knew how serious Ephrem was about selling the map to a worthwhile owner, rather than an Asurian zealot.

Rex nodded solemnly. "Sorry to say how right you are." He collected his rounded ceramic knife and plunged it into Ephrem's arm.

Ephrem stumbled back, painting the floor with the geyser of his own fresh blood.

Rex snatched Ephrem's knife from the counter and threw it. The blade pierced through Ephrem's jacket, making him breathe deep and stumble. Rex ran around the table and shoved it deeper into the other man's chest.

A moment later, Ephrem fell still, wondering just why Rex would attack him before learning how to read the arrows on the map.

Once the storm broke, Rex scrubbed the stained floors. Spilled blood was bad for business and he had two bodies to dispose of before he could reopen the alehouse.

A short-haired couple walked inside, both wearing polished black armor. Luminescent crystal trim twisted in purposeful strokes within the dark coating. Of the couple, the woman carried a halberd; the man carried a sword as long as he was tall. Both placed their weapons by the door before approaching the ale counter.

Rex rose from his cleaning and washed his hands in the basin next to the tap. "Can I interest two of Shabra-Lai's finest in something to drink?"

"Not this time," the woman said.

"We were following a man through the storm," the man said. "He rode a mantorse. It's the same one that's tied outside."

With a nod, Rex said, "He was here. Killed an Asurian right before I killed him." Reaching under the counter, Rex set the roll and crystal glass in front of the duo. "He had these with him."

The duo looked at each other for a long moment before the man got up and walked outside. Still at the counter, the woman said, "This is what we were after."

When the man came back in, he put a woven bag on the counter. "Thank you for protecting the secret of Shabra-Lai."

Rex opened the bag and looked at the gold coins inside. Smirking, he said, "My pleasure."

The woman collected the map and glass, along with her halberd. The man picked up his sword and walked out with his partner.

Once the duo flew away on their dragon, Rex looked through the gold coins. His beard hid the size of his smile, a smile that said he knew where the black dot on the map led. But the knights wouldn't pay for that knowledge in gold, only in blood.

SHADOWS IN PLACE OF LIGHT

Seasons upon seasons back
Whispers of scandal arrived
There was a place in the world
Devoid of light

Not a town shrouded by a storm
Not a dragon basking under a cliff
An entire location
Devoid of light.

It came to pass in ages beyond
Rumors following the world's construction
If respite exists may it be
Devoid of light.

THE MIRROR OF TILA

Imperia Sorcha Kagatsu pushed her lover's body away from her knife. As his body struck the floor, the large man's death coiled around the woman's hand a moment before she absorbed it. She always thought the source of her power looked like a whisper torn from a pool of molten lava.

A spray of crimson struck her hand, shading her fingers the same complexion as her luscious hair. The dead man's blood speckled from the center of her sheets to the edge of the bed. Tossing the blade aside, the Imperia lifted her hands overhead, locking her wrists together. A scarlet drop touched her right cheek, just below her eye.

Gazing overhead, Sorcha proclaimed her fealty, her devotion, her ceaseless faith. "Praise to You, Helio-Asura, Destroyer of all things. Praise the strength you have given me. Praise the Death You bring." For a moment, she lingered in the same pose, staring past her hands. The gleam of the sun overhead filled her spirit, just as her lover's death empowered her body.

A knock on the door pulled the Imperia's attention away from her god. "What is it?"

The door slid open halfway. A wiry young man wearing thin black robes stepped forward, looking down. "I heard a noise, Imperia, and your prayers."

"Beathan has served his purpose," Sorcha said. "My womb is fertile and empowered once again."

"Shall I take Beathan for curing?"

She nodded, flicking her fingers away. "And have fresh bedclothes put in place. I have no desire to sleep in a man's blood."

"It will be done," the young man said.

An array of scrolls and bound volumes covered the table where Sori worked. As she read through a section of text for the eighth time, the young woman absently pulled on her cylindrical cap so she wouldn't touch her oiled black hair.

On the opposite side of the room, Maester Mitchell entered, folding his hands within the sleeves of his thick brown robe. "How goes your studies today?"

Sori stood up and bowed. "Maester. I'm sorry. I didn't see you come in."

"There is nothing to be sorry about," Mitchell said. "I only wanted to check your progress."

"Oh." For a moment, the young woman couldn't breathe. "Well, thank you."

"You are welcome. Now, what have you found on the origins of magic?"

Sori lifted the scroll she'd been reviewing and brought it to her teacher. "In Ancient Asuria, there was a city where much of their history and artifacts were kept, but it was 'removed.' That's the word I keep seeing for it. 'Removed.'"

"You're still certain that Asuria is where magic came to be?"

"If not there, then the answer is there. Rather, it's in this removed city. The Mirror of Tila, the weapon used to force sunlight into the earth? It's supposedly there as well. And there's more." Sori ran back to the table, grinning as she grabbed one of the books. She flipped through the pages as she listed more artifacts. "The First Pyromantic Brand, the Aegis of Ice, there might even be a map to The Night Lands."

"Most of those things are folklore."

"But all folklore starts with some fact, Maester. That's why I keep rereading these accounts. Something happened in Ancient Asuria, in a city that's been removed."

"Do not dwell too closely on such things," Mitchell said. "Holes in folklore, no matter the source, do not often present concrete evidence."

Wearing a red and black dress of the finest dragon weave, the Imperia stepped from her bedchamber. Everyone bowed their heads as she passed. A slight smile touched her face. Her crimson hair shifted, reminding her of the seven-pointed tiara she wore. As she approached the back entrance to the worship chamber, Sorcha tapped one of her talons against the polished bone gage in her right ear.

A pair of red-sashed guards pulled aside the curtains blocking her path. While they lowered their heads, she didn't spare either the slightest gaze.

The Imperia stepped into the worship chamber and climbed her dais. A wide throne of polished dragon bone waited for her. She sat on a white cushion, resting her arms on the curved rests, giving her a more open demeanor. Three rows of generals and ministers knelt at the foot of the dais.

"I have taken Beathan's death into my heart," Sorcha said. "It shall nurture the weak flesh crawling inside me."

In unison, those kneeling said, "Praise the Death He brings."

"We have two, perhaps three seasons before the flesh inside me matures. I want our next expansion underway before then."

One of the black-robed ministers rose for a moment and spoke. "Ancient Asuria has been restored, Imperia. The provincial states have sent offerings and made sacrifices. They are no longer conquered, for they are truly Asurian." He knelt once more.

"I will decide who or what is truly Asurian." Sorcha leaned back in her throne, rubbing the top of her sculpted fingernail so it would polish once more. "Is is not enough for us to restore our traditional borders. The purpose of our faith is to convert everyone, so we might prepare for the Death He brings. Everything must die, for this is where our strength comes from."

A general with two red sashes and cape stood. Her slicked black hair showed off a face tanned and cracked by the constant sun. "Twenty thousand soldiers stand ready to advance, Imperia. They only need a direction to turn." She knelt once more.

"As I was empowered, Helio-Asura made His Will known to me. Our next objective should be a step toward reaching our true faith. Simple expansion will never be enough to take the world, unless we can move without any restriction." Sorcha licked her lips in anticipation, savoring how so many of her servants held their breath while waiting for her to speak. "General, prepare plans for taking Ortica."

The great dragon nest echoed through the air, though never louder than a whisper. "Ortica."

"A converted Ortica will give us control of most air travel. We will no longer be forced to lean on greedy guilds for transport to our holy places."

From the back, a minister stood, holding his arms at his sides. "Imperia, Ortica has a million citizens and a thousand dragon nests. How can this be done?"

Sorcha grinned. "I will use the Mirror of Tila."

In her private study, Sori read over her own notes. A length of dried jerky hung out of the side of her mouth while she absently reviewed her thoughts.

Bounding from the shadows, a bundle of soft fur with a pair of big eyes appeared in her lap. "Mouw?"

Without turning her gaze, the historian stroked her pet. "Hi Ferrix."

"Mouw."

"If someone could find just one of these artifacts, we could double everything we know about Ancient Asuria and the Demon Wars. Just think about it." Sori turned to her pet, scratching the affectionate animal behind its floppy ears. "Somewhere out there is a city cloaked in clouds, hidden off the Ash Coasts—wait."

The historian stood—urging Ferrix to jump down—and crossed the room. Brushing a finger over a polished wooden rack, Sori took out a crude map of Ancient Asuria. Sori traced a finger out of the desert and to the surrounding coastline. She rubbed a path around the sea, never coming to a stop. "There's no volcanic activity near Asuria."

"Mouw?"

"The Ash Coasts are volcanic. Every reference to this removed city says it should be hidden within the clouds. *Acker's History of Tila* says her treasures were lost to an unyielding storm. The Ash Coasts are not known for storms."

Ferrix snuggled against the historian's ankle. "Mouw."

"I know, storms happen everywhere, but where is a storm unyielding?"

Focused on cuddling, the furry beast offered no answer.

"Sometimes, I don't know why I keep you around." She reached down, stroking Ferrix's neck. He lowered both of his ears and relaxed his jaw.

Shaking her head, Sori sat down once more, resuming her reading. Her lips continued to chew on the dried jerky in her mouth, just as her hands continued to stroke Ferrix's thick fur.

∞

Sorcha massaged her lower abdomen. She knew a bump would soon become visible, even without the added pressure of her hand.

A gaunt messenger shuffled into the worship chamber, lifting bony hands while his knobby knees landed on the polished floor. "Praise…" The messenger heaved and slipped so he had to hold himself up with his hands as well. "Praise… the…"

Rolling her eyes, the Imperia released a sharp exhale. "Praise the Death He brings, yes. What do you have to report?"

The messenger wheezed every time he drew in a single breath. "The Mirror. Taken."

Standing, the Imperia asked, "By who?"

"Three defilers. A nimble young woman in green, a spear-wielding mercenary, and an Ortican dragon rider."

Touching the messenger's face, Sorcha took a deep breath. "Send word to the general that I wish to see her." She clawed the messenger's face, shoving the sickly man. Blood speckled onto the sparkling floor. "Tell her what you just told me."

As he cradled the side of his face, the messenger backed away. "Yes, Imperia."

When she was alone, Sorcha knelt beside the spilled blood. She scratched the drops into the outline of the famed peninsula of dragons, whispering its name. "Ortica."

Even in her free time, Sori poured through maps and meteorological records. Ferrix often dashed around her feet, though he never jumped onto the tables. The small creature cared too much for his owners beloved maps and scrolls to do such a thing.

A door opened on the far side of the historian's study chamber, causing the furry beast to charge off and explore. Sori spotted her pet's sudden departure and snapped to her feet. "Ferrix! Come back here." Without putting on her cap, the historian ran after her pet, hoping he hadn't caused any problems. She ran through several rows, catching glimpses of a furry leg or tail just before it slipped out of sight.

Her canvas shoes clopped over the polished floors. Each smooth surface had to be lacquered by acolytes and students. For every eight gales of work they put in, the administrators allowed the neophytes three gales of time to read and study. Only for a few seasons had Sori been exempt from doing any physical labor to support the time she spent on her studies. If Ferrix did anything in the public areas, the administrators would make sure none of the acolytes cleaned up after him.

A small round of barks erupted from behind a row of bookshelves.

"Ferrix. What are you doing?" Sori stepped around the corner and saw a medium-height man with dark eyes and a bright smile. He held up his hands, letting his sleeves dip toward his elbow, much like the hood that had fallen to his shoulders. "Oh, sir. Sorry about that." The historian marched forward and crouched, scooping her pet off the floor.

"Nothing to apologize for." He reached into a travel pack and removed a small nut. Holding it toward Ferrix, he said, "This is for you."

The small beast leaned toward the nut and sniffed it for a moment. Then he grabbed it with his front teeth and pulled the nut away.

"Such a cutie," the man said. "What's his name?"

"Ferrix. I found him when I went on a fishing expedition twelve seasons ago. He usually sticks to tormenting vermin and bugs."

"He didn't torment me at all." The man took a finger and scratched Ferrix behind an ear for a moment. "I'm Toby. Are you Sori?"

The historian's eyes widened. "I am."

"Wonderful. Maester Mitchell said you might be here, and that you might have a little friend."

"Oh. Um, if Maester Mitchell sent you, what can I help you with?"

Toby's smile widened. "I'm trying to find some information about Tila. I'm putting together a history of the last few seasons of her life, when she scattered her weapons between her husbands."

Sori tucked a lock of hair behind her ear lobe. "You've come to the right place."

An Ortican? The notion caused Sorcha's blood to quake in terror, afraid of the fury she might bring. A wordless whisper in her mind restored her composure.

Her general entered the worship chamber and knelt. "Imperia, I await your command."

Sorcha felt the life of her soldier, the beat of the darkened woman's heart, the exchange of breaths as each moment passed.

"I wish to know where I can find this trio." Sorcha approached the center of the room, ignoring the general's direct presence there. Looking up until her eyes filled with Helio-Asura's might, the

Imperia said, "The loyal masses have duties to attend to. For this affront, they will taste my judgment."

"Imperia, I do not wish to offend—"

"Then say nothing."

"Yes, Imperia. It is only that I would not want you to be without servants, should you desire them."

A spark of amusement passed Sorcha's lips as she looked down. "Have a company on alert once the defilers have been tracked down. They will stand ready at a distance." She marched toward her bedchamber, wishing rest before her journey.

The parasite within her squirmed in anticipation.

Rain battered at the fountains next to each window. The Archive would have fresh drink for some time, relying only on the supply provided by the weather. Sori read through an account of Tila's seventh battle in the shadows, a fight shrouded within a long Monsoon.

"Inspired by the weather?" Maester Mitchell asked.

"Somewhat, yes."

"Perhaps it will aid your efforts."

"I hope so as well, Maester."

"Perhaps it will aid you as much as Toby."

Sori nearly laughed. Her right hand snapped over her mouth for an instant.

"There is nothing to worry about," Mitchell said. "We each study in our own way."

The Maester lay a hand on Sori's shoulder and walked away. She returned to her reading long enough for Ferrix to startle her. "Mouw."

The scholar stroked her pet's ears. "What have you been up to, you little scamp?"

"Helping me, actually." Toby approached Sori's table. As he sat, he held out a nut for Ferrix to eat.

Sori leaned back in her chair, crossing her arms. "How has he helped you?"

Toby lay a cracked scroll on the table. "He ambushed me before I could glance past this."

With a gentle touch, she unrolled the parchment. A sketch resembling the continent spread over the sheet, with dozens of points marked, each with a note etched in fine print. "What language is this?" she asked.

"I don't know." Toby pointed at one of the annotated dots resting away from any landmass. "What's this supposed to be?"

Holding her breath, Sori put her head close to the page. "That can't be right."

"What?"

"Mouw?" Ferrix hopped onto the edge of the table and watched the scholar closely.

"This symbol in the center? It's similar to a Pyromantic glyph for 'shield.' That same glyph is used in Dranglei to describe the Mirror of Tila."

"Where is this spot at?" Toby asked. "Compared to where we are now?"

Sori smiled. "I'd have to double check, but I think it's close to Storm Hold."

Every booth rumbled with activity on the mountain spire of Shai Ek. Traders from each direction stood under tents and canopies, exchanging materials for coins, goods for servants. Along the side ridges, several dragons batted each other for any stray bits that might be cast off the peak.

Clad in the violet robes and hood of a Mayok death scribe, Sorcha pressed through the crowd. She searched for anything, any sign of those who had taken her Mirror. A young woman with oiled hair hung on the arm of a middle-aged man, constantly searching for those willing to report a redhead to bounty hunters or Asurians. If the Imperia weren't concealing her identity, she would have told the girl not to bother. Dipping one's hair in black liquid rarely aided anyone, not even Sorcha.

She moved from one stall to the next, looking over goods if she found no one matching the descriptions given by the messenger. A slight girl in green, a rider with a scar over his nose, and a mercenary with a jade crystal spear. Sorcha wondered what punishment best fit their crimes.

Close to a booth, the Imperia made a short stride and approached a man cooking meat and bread. "May your harvest and hunt be plentiful," she said, reciting the complimenting greeting common among Mayok disciples.

"No story to tell here," the man said without looking away from his work.

"Please forgive." Sorcha struggled with the accent, but recalled the cadence of Mayok speakers from her younger days. "My scrolls are filled. Do you know Ortican rider?"

"I know how to crack shells to get to meat. I know how to mix grains and mold. Anything else doesn't pay."

She lowered her head. "May you discover great tales for next meet." As Sorcha turned to leave, she bumped into a man with a white grin contrasting with his sun-scorched skin.

"Careful," he said.

"Much sorry."

Just as the Imperia was about to step away, the grinning man pulled her back. With two fingers, he made a gap between Sorcha's veil and hood. "An Asurian turned Mayoki? Interesting."

"Yes," she said. "Far home. Mother whore. Do you know Ortican rider?"

"Perhaps," the grinning man said while nodding. "Can you convince me to tell you?"

Sorcha lowered her head, pulling her veil back into place. "Yes. Need a private place. Stories are intimate."

He put an arm around her shoulders and guided her onward. "I know a place that might work."

Moments later, the Imperia found herself inside a tent made of thick canvas, capable of blocking most sunlight. The door flap closed, leaving only a small brazier to reveal her surroundings. A water sac, several bulky leather bags, and a torn bedroll.

"Lie down," the man said. "I hope Mayoki like to be ridden."

"Stories are sad and quiet," Sorcha said, sliding onto the bedroll. "Loud stories use skin, not words."

"Shut up." The man moved to push Sorcha flat against the cushion, but she grabbed his wrist.

Her index finger pushed against his eye, pressing between his iris and tear duct. As the man cried blood, the Imperia shifted her fingers. "Tell me what I want to know," she said. "I have no desire for you beyond that."

A cool breeze drifted through Sori's window, drawing her arms around her undressed body. Soon, she knew the heat would fade, leading into the season of Monsoon. Already, she could see thicker clouds in the distance, possibly half a continent away.

"What is it?" Toby asked from under the bed sheets. "I'm not ready to get up yet."

"Monsoon," the scholar said. "I don't know how many gales until the rain starts."

"Didn't we just have Monsoon?"

"Before this Scorch." She pulled the glass shutters inside, blocking out the sudden chill. Rubbing her arms, Sori slipped on her underdress, then pulled on the bed sheets.

Toby sat up, covering his eyes with one hand. "I'm up already."

"I want to go over some scrolls before it gets too humid."

The adventurous man took Sori's hand, guiding her close. His lips pressed soothing warmth into her mouth. A gentle tickle rippled over her spine as his fingers ran over her scalp.

Sori backed away with a smile. "Get dressed. We've got reading to do."

"Sure. You going to touch up your roots first?"

Touching the part in her hair, Sori groaned. "Really? I just did that."

"I like the red."

The scholar pulled a jar of dark liquid from her dresser. "You remember that if that Asurian death cult stops by. They're known for kidnapping redheads."

"You mean ethnic Asurians?"

Sori dipped a fine brush into the jar. "There isn't enough evidence to support that conclusion."

"Then why do you oil your hair?"

"Because such a feature is unbecoming of a scholar," Sori said. "Sameness of appearance helps us focus our minds on that which we research."

Still clad in her false robes, Sorcha followed the once-grinning man. His gaze kept shifting back to the Imperia, his wide iris filled the corner of his eye.

"Keep going," Sorcha said behind her veil.

A massive tent stood ahead. Made of large tan patches sewn together, the tent looked better than any in the Asurian Army from a distance. Even with the piecemeal construction, Sorcha knew it hadn't been made simply for functionality. The entry tunnel stood in place thanks to wide double stitches that reinforced the patched walls and roof flap.

Inside the inner flap, the Imperia saw a dragon laying on the far side of the tent. All four of the thick black and red wings lay folded against the dragon's semi-armored hide. Ropes behind the slumbering creature tied down a wide section of the tent. Several traders lined the path leading to the great beast. Several drooling milk beasts wandered past with a quartet of hoofed pups racing to catch up.

To the far left, several gamblers assembled around a bowl-shaped dice table. Among those present was a slight girl smoking a pipe, her clothes were different shades of green.

Beside the dragon, a man in Ortican armor took notes from a line of beckoners. Such dragon riders could pick and choose their clients. Everyone paid the fees to fly. Strapped to the dragon's passenger harness, an oval-shaped bundle of canvas rested against the beast's side.

"No," the mercenary carrying a spear said. He looked through a bin of fruit while a small man with one arm questioned him.

"I have money. You could find and kill the raiders before the others leave. It'll take nine gales for you at the most."

"No."

Sorcha could have reached out and ended the mercenary first, but she wanted her property back first. A big display would make it harder for her to approach the dragon.

Poking her reluctant guide in the back, the Imperia said, "Go to the rider. Push the others in line aside."

"But—"

She pressed her fingernail into the man's skin. "Your death can power me, or you can do as I say."

The once-grinning man moved forward. When he reached the line, he started pushing people to the left and right so he might pass.

Sorcha followed the forced disruption. "Excuse," she said. "Most sorry. Please sorry."

As the line gave way to the once-grinning man's advance, the dragon rider stood. "I should cut you down right now."

"Don't bother," Sorcha said. She clawed her reluctant guide's neck, forcing him to cower in pain. "I want what is mine." The Imperia removed her veil, allowing a lock of crimson hair to tumble freely beside her face. She pointed at the oval parcel mounted on the dragon's side.

A stick struck Sorcha's side. She looked to the right out of reflex. The embers of a smoking pipe lit the hem of her false robes on fire.

While she stamped out the flames, a female voice yelled. "Bloodwing, move! It's the Imperia!"

The girl in green rammed into Sorcha, knocking the Imperia to the dirt. The dragon rider jumped onto his steed.

"Storytellers don't walk like they own the world," the girl in green said.

The dragon jumped to its feet, crashing through the wide panel of the tent.

"Fair point," Sorcha said. She pressed the tips of her fingernails into the palm of her right hand. When she opened her hand, a concussive wave erupted around her, throwing people and produce through the air, eventually ripping the tent in a dozen different places.

∞

Ferrix dashed around Sori and Toby, hopping at times with glee. The scholar shifted her pack, unused to having so much weight pulling at her shoulder. "Are you sure your friend will be there on time?"

"Yes," Toby said. He adjusted his own travel bag to rest around both of his shoulders. "She's an excellent rider, one of Ortica's best."

"As long as she can get us there and back." Ferrix jumped into Sori's arms. "It'd be nice if she were punctual too."

Toby laughed. "Relax. She'll be there."

"Sorry. I just don't want the Maesters to catch us in the rain."

"Does Mitchell go out in the rain that often?"

Sori shook her head.

"Then I wouldn't worry."

At the end of the entry hall, the rupturing roar of thunder tried to ward Sori from her adventure. She'd never done anything daring in her life, not even a slight act of rebellion toward her tutors.

The scholar tucked her pet into the largest of her robe's pockets. She dropped a bit of jerky in as well before tying the pocket shut. Toby glanced at the new cloth bulge. "What?" Sori asked. "You don't expect me to leave him pining at the gates for me to come back."

He shrugged. "Guess not. Maybe he'll sniff out some treasure when we get there."

Together, they pushed against one of the gates. Wind and cold drops of water blasted inward. Lightning flared the darkened sky back to light once again. The thick wooden barrier swung outward, sending a thicker coat of moisture over Sori and Toby.

Outside, they both pulled on the door, which snapped shut in an instant. Toby said something, but the roaring wind crushed the sound of his words. A moment later, he pointed at the sky above.

A dragon glided downward with all four of its wings spread wide. The air caused the membranes to billow like a cloth. The blue-green creature carried a swaying basket between its feet. When the dragon flew low, Toby pointed at the basket.

Sori nodded in response. She knew they would have to jump aboard the basket. So much precipitation made a full landing far too dangerous, especially with the chance the dragon might lose a membrane when it touched the ground. Regardless of the weather, the scholar dreamed of having a dress made from the naturally-grown cloth.

A dash forward pushed Sori through curtains of rain. Ferrix squirmed inside her pocket. The scholar put her hand over the pocket, hoping to console her pet if she couldn't console herself.

Toby grabbed the edge of the basket, hanging on with one hand while reaching back with the other. Running off excitement and her faith in Toby, Sori raced onward. Her eyes stayed shut through her sprint, opening only to make sure she continued moving toward the dark blur just outside her reach.

A cold, hard grip locked around her wrist. Pain cracked through her muscles. The scholar screamed as Toby pulled her into the basket.

Sori cradled her arm while Toby pulled the woven door shut. Inside her pocket, Ferrix asked, "Mouw?" She had no answer.

Drips of rain eased through the woven reeds of the basket. Winds thrashed at the small capsule, causing Sori to creep into Toby's arms. For a moment, she considered loosening her robes so he might take her away from her fear for a few moments. The trip would take long enough, especially since no dragon could fly high enough to go over the clouds approaching Storm Hold. Heat from the sun would scorch anyone who tried into instant ashes.

In the constant shaking, she could feel Ferrix curl into a ball and huddle next to her hip. She did not know how to calm him since she could not fully calm herself.

Then calm. Peace. Hardly a drop of moisture tried to penetrate the basket. Nothing swayed the small craft through the air.

"Think we're there?" Toby asked.

Ferrix stuck his head out of the scholar's pocket, gazing around. "Mouw. Mouw."

Sori scratched her friend's ears. "We might be." She crawled to the edge of the basket, easing the hatch open.

They flew within a bubble of calm. Beyond a dense wall of clouds, the pale blue dragon's wings relaxed as they approached a derelict city half buried within a mountain-sized boulder. The tops of towers had cracked, some broke enough to lose their angular tips ages in the past. Only a central ringed building had not crumbled during the passage of endless seasons.

Their dragon came down, landing hard in an open plaza a short distance from the ringed building. A guttural cry erupted from the beast that had carried them. Sori looked out, seeing a large azure sheet drifting over an expansive path of broken stones.

Holding out her hand, Sori counted the drops of moisture landing in her palm. There were only two.

"It's much drier here than I expected," Toby said.

A still hum rumbled from the surrounding cloud wall. For a moment, it sounded like thunder, but continued too long and steady. No light ruptured through the condensed precipitation, even as the sound grew louder. Within the torrent of sound, Sori heard a word, perhaps a name. "Kagatsu."

"What's that?" Sori asked. "Kagatsu?"

Toby's eyebrows lifted high and his eyes widened. "I'm not sure."

"Really? Doesn't mean anything to you?"

"Not really, no—"

The dragon bleated out a high-pitch wail before thrashing its wings randomly. After fumbling for a moment, the rider fell from her steed, her body slapping hard onto the brick path below.

In the cloud wall, dozens and dozens of shapes emerged from brownish gray ripples. Each drifted toward the city, making the torrent grow ever louder.

Once more, Sori heard the name in her mind. "Kagatsu."

The shapes loomed closer. A few surrounded the dragon, pressing through its scales and armor without leaving a mark. More bleating filled the air, sounds easily drowned out by the approaching wraiths.

Sori glanced forward, looking at the ringed building. Grabbing Toby's arm, she said, "Let's go."

"But, Maddie…"

The scholar glanced at the rider. Faintly human shapes surrounded the dark-skinned woman. Each pressed into and through her skin, causing her to scream, then collapse.

Sori looked toward the open doorway ahead. Ferrix shifted in her pocket, curling into a tight, shivering ball.

With the droning growing ever louder, the scholar moved faster, dragging her companions onward.

After running through several curved doors, Sori stopped in a near-abyssal room. The only light came from behind them.

Toby held up a long stick that burst with light at the tip.

"What was that?" Sori asked.

"This is a plume torch. No fire—"

"I meant the…" She gestured at the door they'd come through. "Whatever that is. What were those things?"

"I don't know."

"Don't give me that." She shoved Toby with both hands, making him tumble backward onto a brick floor. A cloud of dust billowed upward, making Sori cough. Once her lover stood up, the scholar said, "When they get closer, I hear that name again. Kagatsu."

"What's that mean?"

Sori threw her hands up in the air. "That's what I want to know. They get closer, I hear that name. In my head." She took in a long breath. "It's going to start again soon enough."

A dull hum shook in Sori's mind, forcing her to grasp her forehead.

Toby put a hand on the woman's shoulder. "What's happening?"

"Sharp pain." She gritted her teeth.

He waved the plume torch upward, making a trio of dust crusted gems glisten. "This room is an amplifier."

"Kagatsu."

"I hear them again," Sori said.

Three of the wraiths pressed through the walls, their wispy arms reaching toward the duo.

"Mouw," Ferrix said.

"Yes," the scholar said. "Run."

Sorcha let her false robes fall behind her. If she was to fight in public, she preferred others see who and what she truly was. Concealing the truth would only conceal the faith she meant to instill within any observers.

The rider swooped toward the Imperia, but refused to unleash the beast's breath

The Imperia spread her fingers wide and stared into the palms of her hand. "Let rider and steed feel as one," Sorcha said. "That which touches one shall touch the other in kind." Veins of crimson, purple, and black rose from the Imperia's fingers, swirling through the air as she reached out at her enemy.

"She's attacking Bloodwing," the slight girl in green said. The girl tossed a small blade at Sorcha, causing the Imperia to take a sudden step back.

The mercenary thrust his spear at Sorcha from the opposite side. His large arms tensed as he spun the jade staff. Veins of magic drifted out of the air, swirling around the mercenary's weapon.

Sorcha hurled her black cape at the mercenary, tangling the dragon weave around the spear. The Imperia lunged forward, slashing with the long talons on the tips of her fingers.

"Take the Mirror and go," the mercenary said.

Looking behind her, Sorcha saw the slight girl running toward the dragon.

The mercenary locked his spear around the Imperia, bracing her arms and body against his own chest.

"A pity," Sorcha said, grunting as she tried to pull her arms free.

The mercenary wrapped his left leg around Sorcha's. "Give it up, lady."

"Why?" She curled her fingers—and her fingernails. Grabbing at the mercenary, her talons pierced his armor, digging deeper each second. When she heard an empty moan from the large man's chest, she knew she'd dug deep enough. His grip grew weak, causing him to lose his grip on the spear.

As she stepped away from the mercenary, Sorcha flared her fingers at the crowd. Her wrath twisted like a drill, eating through a pair of spectators in an instant. Death surged in the Imperia's blood, forcing the veins in her eyes to grow thicker and dark like her hair.

Before the dragon could flee with its passengers, several fiery bursts streaked across the sky. A smile warped the corners of the Imperia's mouth as she congealed the mortal suffering into her hands. Her servants fired further attacks, making sure the dragon did not escape.

The beast's quartet of eyes turned toward Sorcha. It breathed steam from the nostrils on its forehead while it turned toward the Imperia. A roar erupted from its mouth as it swooped downward, plasma dripped from its jaws.

Sure of what would come next, the Imperia stretched her arms and clasped the edges of her cape. She took a moment to glance again at the approaching dragon, watching as more plasma curdled behind its angular teeth. Sorcha crouched and lowered her head. Her arms crossed, drawing the onyx weave over her head and shoulders. With her body wrapped, she felt only a small measure of heat as the dragon blasted at her.

She held her breath and started to count. Six breaths and the dragon would need to inhale once more. If it carried on longer, Sorcha's cape would cook under the heat. Her last cape could endure ten breaths of exposure to an attack before the heat penetrated the weave.

The Imperia took small steps forward as quick as she could. Any movement would cut down her exposure to the dragon's plasma. The natural swooping pattern of the weave began to glow, showing Sorcha exactly where the cape would rip open first. Her skin would bear the same patterns for only an instant before the end.

Four breaths passed. Her wrist burned as the count hit five. It was rare for her to think her advisers knew better, but the blister on her arm made her regret deciding to keep her protectors at a distance.

Eight breaths. Sorcha knew this dragon was something else, strong. Why else would she covet having legions of her own to command?

Another way existed to prolong her endurance. She could draw on the power stored inside her. If she had a knife, she could even charge herself with the parasite twisting in her womb.

Releasing her cape, the Imperia rose. Her left hand touched the plasma directly. Rather than scream, she locked her teeth together as the flame ate through muscle and bone. Just as her fingers became a torch, Sorcha swept her left hand in a circle. A ring of death collected the incoming plasma, casting it away from her for an instant.

She raised her right hand, flicking the tips of her fingers enough to block her view of the rider. In one moment, she heard a man scream in pain, a sound blocked half an instant later by the bleating dragon.

The dragon crashed onto a pair of tents, sending shoppers fleeing back into the open. Sorcha's left hand twitched as threads of death chased the people before entering her own body.

Plasma had charred her hair, rendering the back of her head into a light crisp. The stink of her locks irritated her more than the agony ripping through her left arm. She spat to the side, noting how the waves in her cape still glowed from the dragon's attack.

Both tents thrust upward as the dragon rose once more. The rider sat laxed in his saddle, extending a whip at his side.

Everything dead inside Sorcha pooled in her right hand. She glared for an instant at the rider, then whipped her eyes upward at the dragon's snarling face.

Another pool of plasma filled the dragon's mouth. Sorcha snapped her right hand to point at the liquid embers. Her might erupted, blasting as a single bolt into the dragon's head.

A fleshy pop dropped the beast's neck while chunks of bone and meat rained onto ground.

The fingers of Sorcha's left hand closed into a fist. Ashen scales cracked apart as the limb restored underneath.

The slight girl in green tumbled off the dragon's back, dragging the wrapped parcel behind her. She noticed the Imperia's approach before tripping over her own ankle.

Sorcha shambled to the girl, collapsing on top of her. They wrestled for a moment before the Imperia locked the long nails of her right hand around jade-clad woman's throat.

A group of Asurian soldiers filled the ruined shopping area. Two stopped behind Sorcha, clasping their fists against their chests. "Imperia, we have secured the marketplace."

"Good," she said. "Take this one into custody along with her confederates. I still haven't decided what to do with them."

Dust in the sacrificial chamber curled with the wind, forming miniature dunes in the stone floor. Bits of ancient tapestries mixed with the detritus in the room, leaving shredded half-emblems on the wall.

On the opposite side of a long altar, a gray shroud stood in a corner, stained with streaks of bricks eroded from the ceiling above.

Sori ignored the sweat draining from her brow down to her legs. Instead, she fixated on the shroud. Her shoes plowed over the dunes, leaving prints on stones that had been untouched for millions upon millions of seasons. The scholar touched the thick cloth, pulling it downward. Her heart beat thinking about what she might soon lay her eyes upon.

The cloth crumbled in her hands, breaking into a hundred dusty clumps. A layer of eroded remains covered the large oval mounted atop a stone dais. Sori pressed her hand against the smooth surface.

Drawing in a deep breath, the scholar began to loosen the restraint held on all her knowledge. "It was said, in ancient times, that Tila was born in a city by the sea. During a Monsoon, the rain broke and her neighbors dashed out to fish during the calm. Once everyone had their lines in place, the sun shook and a section of it fell."

Toby glanced back the way they'd come. "What are you going on about?"

Sori pushed her hand downward, clearing the smooth pane of dust. The particles fell from the bottom of the oval in a sheet of sprinkles. Under the scholar's hand, the material tingled with cold, though it did not chill her. "When that piece of the sun fell, it plunged the region into darkness," Sori said. "Even with a lingering echo sunlight overhead, there was largely darkness. The seasons moved differently there, motivated by cold rather than heat. The survivors called it 'night.'"

"Is this going to help us against those wraiths?"

"Yes," Sori said, though she didn't turn away from the oval, instead clearing more of the ancient dust away. When she saw her reflection, the scholar continued her history. "Some of the survivors became curious once the dark settled in. Even with scarce light, they wanted to know what had fallen from the sky. What they found was a material that was neither metal nor crystal. It was luminous, yet held no light of its own.

"Like many of her neighbors, Tila took a section of the material for her own. Not long after, demons rose from the earth, giant monsters determined to crush humanity. Most died. Tila, taking a few belongings, fled."

Steps echoed outside the chamber as several people drew closer. "We don't have much time," Toby said.

Sori put a hand on each side of the freshly cleaned surface. "In time, Tila realized when light touched the piece of fallen sky, the Mirror would glow with untold intensity. This became the strongest weapon of her age, the Mirror of Tila."

"Is that the Mirror? Can we use it against those wraiths?"

"I think so. They seem allergic to direct light."

"I see."

Instead of wraiths, the other members of their expedition came in, even those who'd been attacked by the ghastly forms. They all drew clubs and walked past Toby. The handsome adventurer pulled out a bludgeon of his own. "I know you won't submit," he said. "So you'll have to be prepared."

Clubs struck Sori's head and arms, then she saw nothing more.

Asurian soldiers shoved the trio of thieves to their knees while more fighters inventoried the goods on hand. Sorcha crossed her arms in front of her chest, glaring down at the three.

First she approached the mercenary, the man who'd fought so closely with her. "You have strength and skill. You were the best chance your group had for success." She was lying, but it was part of her way. They needed to accept her word as the only true reality. "Have you anything to say for yourself?"

He stared up at the Imperia. "It was a job." His voice remained even, steady. "I was paid to start the job. I'll be paid again when I finish it."

"So even and bold." Sorcha nodded. Her left hand pointed down at the mercenary while her right pointed to several soldiers standing to the side. "Castrate this man and give him to the army. Let them have their way with him."

The cluster of soldiers surrounded the mercenary, striking him with the dull ends of their spears. Several hits struck the large man's head, drawing blood from his brow. Once the mercenary's struggling grew weak, the soldiers drug him away, pulling him by both arms.

"Who wants to go next?" Sorcha looked at the slight girl, then shook her head. Seeing the dragon rider's slumped posture, the Imperia knew this was the time to strike. "You, rider. Your heart aches for the death of your beast."

He didn't answer, only staring where his mount's body was taken apart so every scrap of it could be used.

"Speak. You ache for your pet."

"Zarras…"

"Pledge yourself to Asuria and I will see to it that you fly again."

The rider looked up. "There's no sense in riding without her."

"Very well." Sorcha snapped her fingers under the rider's chin, her fingernails punctured his neck. Blood ran down his chest while his breathing turned to gurgles. With his will to live drained, the Imperia siphoned less death from the man than she'd hoped.

Sorcha turned to the last of her enemies, the slight girl in green. "I take it from your silence and your gear that you're a survivalist."

"Yes," the girl in green said.

"If it's possible, do you intend to survive this meeting?"

"Anything can be survived."

"I see." The Imperia paced around her prey, looking over the girl's slight form. "You remind me of a historian I encountered a few seasons before I restored Asuria as a single nation."

"Did you feed her to your troops?"

Softly, Sorcha said, "No. She was far too important for that." The Imperia ran her fingers over the surface of the Mirror. "Without her, I would never have found the Mirror in the first place."

"You think you're some reincarnation of Tila, don't you?"

Sorcha glanced over her shoulder. "I could have been. I decided to be something more." She stepped in front of the survivalist and grabbed her thick brown hair by the scalp. With a lift, the Imperia pulled the girl in green in front of the Mirror, then dropped her over an arm's length in front of the reflective surface.

"The Mirror of Tila is a great weapon," Sorcha said as she stood behind the bound young woman. "On a large scale, it can destroy so much."

The Imperia pressed the tips of her fingernails against the survivalist's temples. Pressing against the rugged skin drew a single bead of blood on each side.

"On a personal scale, the Mirror allows one to reflect on themselves in profound ways. A single glance can make the meek discover the power of our god."

Gritting her teeth, the slight girl said, "I'm not one of your followers."

Sorcha pressed her fingers in deeper, burying the length of her nails and her fingertips within the young woman's skull. The slight girl opened her mouth and widened her eyes in a silent gasp.

"Perhaps not, but you did say that anything can be survived."

When Sori opened her eyes again, she found herself strapped to a stone slab. Overhead, an opening pointed up to the sun, though it remained obscured by storm clouds. Glancing down, she saw her robes had been removed, replaced with a pair of sheer strips of cloth.

A wraith rippled above the historian, gazing close with its faceless void. Where a person would have fingers, the spectral figure's limbs drifted into ever-thinning clouds. Past Sori's head, a desiccated body lay in state, having been so long dried out that it lacked any clear gender.

Trails of moisture wisped over the stone under Sori's head. Each wet streak trailed a swirl of black from where someone had washed the oil out of the historian's hair.

"There was no need for you to hide your hair color," Toby said. "It proves your heritage so we can restore your birthright."

"Please," Sori said. "Let me go."

"You'll release yourself in a short while. There's nothing for you to fear."

"I don't want to die."

"We will all die in service to Helio-Asura or in the Offering of Final Death. You have nothing to fear from us. Soon, we will serve you."

"I'll do whatever you want," the historian said. A bead of sweat rolled off her brow. "Just please don't do this."

Toby clapped a hand over Sori's mouth. "Hush. This is empowerment."

The restraints pull right, holding Sori to the slab tighter than before. She glanced past her head as much as she could, seeing a desiccated arm rise only for the limb to break into dust.

Toby slashed his palm, pouring fresh blood onto Sori's face. The historian shook her head in disgust and reflex. Dust particles in the air began to swirl over Sori, curling into a vortex leading to blood anointing her face.

To the side, the wraith reached for the vortex. Its arm became tangled with the vortex of dust, drawing further inside with each passing moment.

Sori heard a whisper, though came from no direction at all. "Sou Kagatsu," was all the whisper said. A name, one the historian might have checked against the records if she hadn't been offered as a sacrifice to the Asurian sun god.

Opposite the wraith and vortex, Toby extended his arms and dropped his knife. He looked upward and said, "Praise the Death He brings."

From behind the man, a dark-skinned arm pulled Toby's head back. Using a chipped combat blade, the priest's attacker slashed his throat, opening a shower of blood over Sori's face and chest.

More dust blew over the historian's flesh, sticking to her wherever Toby's blood struck her body. The vortex began to shimmer with a hollow glow, boring into Sori's abdomen.

The wraith started losing its shape, fading into nothing more than a thin fog.

The Asurian warrior dropped Toby's body and wiped her knife over Sori's cheeks. The historian cried out as more frantic sweat tumbled from her face.

A wash of light struck her. The dust was gone. The wraith no longer stood next to her. Even the warrior stepped away from her altar.

No one spoke. None of the remaining wraiths approached. Even the wind outside stopped moving.

Sori pulled against her restraints, pleading for them to release her. Each line held, but she felt her wrists moving inside each loop. Her blood ran warm, but not enough to burn her. The sensation surged around her arms and legs until a snap echoed four times to release her.

The historian sat up, clutching the slight strips of fabric against her body. No one approached to fasten the restraints once more. Somehow, the nail extending from every digit had grown as long as the attached finger.

An invisible wave rose from the fresh corpse, surrounding Sori. Her hands twisted and curled within the wave, slowly absorbing the sensation into her core.

Though it was death, the sensation filling Sori made her heart race, drove her muscles to light on fire. Her bones became a hidden torch, lighting the way for the power to flow through her. A stroke of contact erupted between her legs and flowed in two lines under her chest. With her birthright flowing about her, the historian knew she could do more, be more than a simple girl looking through books, hoping to discover hidden truths about the past.

What, she wondered, would Tila have done?

The Mirror stood opposite from the window looking out at the storms. Seeing her elongated nails, Sori knew that something in her had changed, aside from all her realizations. Her natural hair color swept over her shoulders and peeked from behind her back.

A tickle touched her bare ankle and she heard a single sound. "Mouw?"

"Ferrix?"

Sori lifted her pet, rubbing his fur so her fingernails wouldn't poke the animal's skin. The soft fur pleasantly rubbed against her skin, just as Ferrix nuzzled his chin over the historian's wrist. She could feel his heartbeat, much like it was her own. His heartbeat linked to her, just as a dozen quiet echoes throbbed around her.

Beyond the Asurians surrounding her, Sori could sense more, faint sparks popping in the distance, even beyond the eternal sun.

Looking up, she could imagine the souls moving on the opposite side of the sun. Gazing up at Helio-Asura, she could feel the most distant bodies more than those close to her.

A single glance brought her back to the Mirror. In her reflection, she longed to see more than what she was. Sori needed to see someone just as capable, if not more, than Tila.

The voice in her mind spoke again. "Kagatsu."

She wanted to stand taller. Power from Toby's death surged through her, elongating her body, so she stood as high as anyone else in the room.

Her figure was too lean and not as enticing as other women. Again the power flowed, pushing through her until there were curves in her hips and a matching slope in her bust.

"You can be Tila," the voice inside her said.

No, Sori thought. I want to be more.

As her jaw shifted forward, removing her slight overbite, depletion and emptiness caught up with her. Sori started to shrink, not just in height, but in the sculpt of her flesh.

"Be more," the voice said. "Be Kagatsu and be anything."

Ferrix snuggled against Sori's arm, rubbing his face against her bare skin. The historian only felt cold, lonely.

"Be Kagatsu. Feel warmth, life, love. Kagatsu."

In a whisper, Sori said, "Yes."

The wraith inside her expanded, looking through her eyes, feeling through her hands. Everything filled with life and warmth once more, just like when she broke her restraints. Sori thought to herself, There is no wraith, there is only me.

Her reflection changed again, but Sori still saw only the flaws in her appearance. Without thinking, she sunk her fingers into Ferrix's skin.

"Mouw! Mouw! Mouw!" None of the sounds stopped Sori's hands.

Gazing into her own eyes, the historian felt the sensation of all the living beings around her. The pleasing memory of being bound to every being around her turned her eyes upward. "I understand," she said. "Praise the Death He brings."

Sori snapped Ferrix's neck, allowing his death to flow into her. She took in an exhilarated breath and continued remaking herself. The historian stopped being an average height slim beacon of cuteness. She wanted to be a vixen, her desire to be adored overflowed as her face changed from that of a simple scholar into the visage of a statuesque seductress.

Tearing away the fur of her pet, Sori turned to the others. "It is done. I know who and what I am now."

"What are you?" the warrior woman asked.

"Your Imperia, inheritor of the Kagatsu bloodline, and highest priestess of Helio-Asura."

Kneeling, the Asurians said, "Hail, Imperia Sori Kagatsu."

"No." The Imperia tore some of the raw meat from the animal's body. Its nourishment would fuel her growing powers further. "Sori is a familiar term for those who I would befriend. Since you are meant to follow me, you shall use my full name—Sorcha Kagatsu."

The Asurians called out their leader's name as she devoured the remains of her pet.

Followed only by a few guards, Sorcha walked through the halls of the archive. The annals that once seemed so great to her had changed into minor scribblings made by inexperienced snobs. For so long, she wanted to be one of them. The Imperia laughed under her breath, confident that she could see how small her former mentors truly were.

Ahead, weathered down by long seasons of age and solitude, Maester Mitchell stood over a bound volume.

Pulling her black cape over her chest, Sorcha approached her former mentor. "There is nothing in there that will give you clarity."

His head lifted slightly before he turned. "That voice. I feel like I should know you."

"Perhaps you should. Perhaps not." The Imperia found herself looking into the Maester's eyes. When they'd last met, the scholar stood taller than his pupil. After so many seasons, Sorcha found herself elevated above the Maester. "You arranged for those thieves to steal my Mirror."

"I do not consort with thieves." Mitchell shifted to face the Imperia. "Who are you?"

"A confused Imperia."

"Imperia?"

"Mine is the hand that guides all of Asuria. However." She touched a long talon to her bottom lip. "My confusion comes from the testimony from one of my most devoted followers." Sorcha waved her fingers, signaling her followers. "Why don't we allow the two of you to discuss the matter."

A woman in layers of pure white walked past the Asurian guards and approached the Imperia. Sorcha shifted a few fingers and the woman in white knelt before drawing back her veil. Mignon looked out with a wide stare and a smile. A single gem of pure white lay fixed on the center of her forehead.

Maester Mitchell looked at the young woman vacantly. He shook his head. "I don't understand."

"Praise the Death He brings," Mignon said. "I told the Imperia everything, Maester. She captured us and enlightened me."

"You were supposed to find the Mirror of Tila."

"And any sign of the student, Sori." Sorcha smirked at her own remark, appreciating the irony of it. "You chose your servants well, Maester. They were successful for a time."

"You should leave your murderous ways in the past, Asurian."

"There was a time when I agreed with you." Sorcha stepped closer to Maester Mitchell. "Back when I oiled my hair to hide my lineage. Thank you for sending Toby to me. If it wasn't for him, I would never have embraced my heritage and found my faith."

"Sori?" The Maester shook his head. "No, you can't be."

"True. I can't be Sori, because I'm so much more. It's a pity you had to try and steal my Mirror. You might have made a worthwhile adviser Illumina, give me his death."

Mignon stood, briefly lowering her head. "Yes, Imperia." She drew a small knife from her belt and prowled toward Mitchell.

Backing away, the elder scholar held up his hands in defense. "We can talk about this, Sori. There's no need to kill me."

"My name," the Imperia said, "is Sorcha. And we all die. It is what Helio-Asura demands of us."

Mignon continued pursuing Maester Mitchell until the older man fell. After a few screams, Sorcha could feel a surge of power enter her limbs and flood into her chest.

Upon her return to Asuria, the Imperia gave the order. Without any fanfare, the first waves of her followers moved out, with Mignon among them. They would whisper into the ears of the influential and the weak. In a season or two, the military would move, this time carrying the Mirror of Tila so Sorcha might use it in battle.

As long as the trip had taken, the Imperia's body had expanded. She'd rarely allowed herself to advance to such a point. A pampered lifestyle did not appeal to her.

The strain had tested the limits of Sorcha's power, enough for her to touch her personal reserves. Everything granted to her from Beathan's death was gone, leaving her with only one other option.

Knowing the price for power was a fearsome knowledge. The Imperia's servants understood why she did some things, but couldn't comprehend the sensations that filled her before she acted.

"It is not an easy thing to guide everyone to devotion and death," she said. Sorcha stood exposed to the sun, but did not look to her god. "Sometimes, we must deprive ourselves of the simplest pleasures if we are to continue to serve."

Lifting the same knife she'd used on Beathan, the Imperia pierced her own side. Groaning, she shoved the tip toward the center of her abdomen before twisting it around. Each subtle motion turned her stomach colder. When she buckled to her knees, the blade moved deeper into her side.

A rush of power flowed through her body, setting her blood vessels on fire. With the cold vanquished from her chest, Sorcha pulled the knife away. A brush of her talons sealed the wound without any scarring. Once she slept, she would discharge the waste and reap another flush of power.

Until then, she planned to sleep, basking in the light of her god.

A SMILE UPON THE SUN

Pay the piper
Settle the score
Give us hope
Forevermore
Ever make Joy
beyond

Shoot a flare
Against a storm
A Smile Upon The Sun

Will you give us
A choice for true
Sing about
Forevermore
Dear hope for your
Love be true

Shoot a flare
Against a storm
A Smile Upon The Sun

Burp that baby
Make em coo
Daring do
Forevermore
Raise em right
Whatever you do

Shoot a flare
Against a storm
A Smile Upon The Sun

When you recall
An entire life
Tell it full
Forevermore
On the pyre
Fly the wind

Shoot a flare
Against a storm
A Smile Upon The Sun

THE TALE OF THE THROAT SLASHER

Skin and cartilage alike fought the passage of Vanity's blade. She knew the moment always came when every natural resistance asserted itself. Even volunteers resisted at that moment, denying the divinity hovering overhead.

Vanity did not look at the body she worked on. Her fingers tightened around her hook-tipped blade, her free hand tugged on a mass of curly locks.

On the opposite side of the room, the Dancer still glared at her.

"I take no joy in this," Vanity said. Blood poured over her knuckles, the death inside raced into her body. A slight tingle washed over the right half of her face.

The Dancer refused to speak, even though Vanity allowed that one area to remain unbound.

Cords of brown leathered coiled around Vanity's captive. The Dancer hung in mid-air, a cord pulled tight against each limb. Further ropes pulled the Dancer's fingers open and apart. A knot of ropes tied the Dancer's blue and purple dreadlocks to the rafters around the central skylight. Rays of sunlight clashed with the Dancer's shredded dress and painted face.

"I am not here to hurt you." Cupfuls of blood lurched over Vanity's blade. The moment of resistance had ended. Vanity breathed deep and relaxed just as the body in front of her relaxed and ceased to breathe.

Withdrawing her blade, Vanity took care to keep the fatal blood away from her silks. She never allowed a drop to touch the pure white or silver trim of her clothing. As Illumina, her duty was to glow as bright as the sun eternally overhead. In two smooth strokes with a rag, the knife was clean, leaving her hands and hair to bear the deep shade of red.

And still, the Dancer did not speak.

Vanity slipped the knife into a bone sheath, then held it out for her spearman Jes to take. The gaunt man took the weapon, then stepped back to the faint shading at the edge of the room.

"There's no reason for us to be enemies. I've come to this city to help you. You're here to defend the people who live here."

The Dancer continued staring at Vanity. Tension never entered or abandoned the Dancer's azure gaze.

Frowning, Vanity turned, pacing up and down the length of the room. The curious sound of shoes echoed her steps just as the hardened soles pinched her toes together. After Vanity turned around twice, a thunderous clip snapped the Dancer's attention.

"Perhaps I should explain myself," Vanity said. "There was a time when I was a lesser creature and only the power of an Asurian could make me whole."

In the time before, her face had been crafted from candle wax then held to a flame. Her left eye sat in the center of her cheek, the corner of her mouth drooped toward her chin.

She pulled her arms against the grip of the spearman who drug her into the chamber. Ahead, brilliant light washed over the room, leaving the outline of a dark-clad figure waiting.

Within the chamber, the spearman tossed her to the floor. A calloused bronze foot pressed onto her hand while a sultry voice spoke. "Thank you, Jes, that will be all."

The spearman's head bobbed down for a moment before he backed out of the door, sealing the stone slab behind him.

Just as she looked up, the Imperia pulled her foot away. "Appearances are an important thing," the woman in black dragon weave said. "Those who serve me must know I am firm and unforgiving."

Atsuko stumbled to her feet, rushing toward the door. The slab did not budge.

"Already fleeing and you haven't even asked the obvious questions."

Lifting an eyebrow, Atsuko looked over her shoulder. The Imperia took a few steps toward her but made no aggressive motions.

"Don't you want to know why I had you brought here?"

Atsuko's lips parted, but she had no answer. The Imperia stood quiet, shifting the obscene talons on the tips of her fingers.

Shaking her head, Atsuko said, "No."

The Imperia smiled. "Yes, you do. Or maybe you know already." Black talons rose to the side of Atsuko's face, brushing against the deformed skin, the edge of the distorted eye socket. "Do you think I feel sorrow or disgust for your malady?"

Atsuko knew the response but had no desire to give the Imperia the satisfaction.

"I'm content to go back to slashing for the mages."

The Imperia pulled her hand away, letting her smile dissolve. "Our God has seen you and would give you purpose."

Scowling, Atsuko turned around. Her fingers curled into fists. "I don't need purpose, Imperia."

Amber lips scowled under a crimson mane and an onyx tiara. "I was not mandated to allow you a choice."

The tips of each talon sank into the left side of Atsuko's face. Heat swelled under her eye, blistering toward her mouth. Atsuko screamed and fell.

Heat faded. Her breathing steadied. Far, far overhead, the sun beamed downward without pause.

The Imperia stepped over Atsuko, blocking out the light. She held out a wide pane of reflective glass. "Look and understand."

Dingy clothes and red hair looked familiar, but the face was a mystery. The woman Atsuko saw was far too symmetrical in expression.

"You were the girl with the melted face?"

The Dancer's sudden question snapped Vanity's eyes open wide. For a moment, Vanity felt the weight of the mass of wavy hair holding down her head. After an instant, she remembered her role and stood tall once again.

"I was born with a disfigurement, yes. Now, I am closer to purity and perfection. All it cost me was--"

"Your soul."

Vanity's mouth snapped into a frown. She tensed her full lips, remembering the agony of their creation. "How could I sell the core of myself?"

"You're the one who sold it. You tell me."

Vanity's fingers tightened together. Since her inclusion, she had not thrown a punch, but the memory was still there. A girl who had to fight off social predators never forgot how to protect herself. "I did not sell my soul. I found myself."

"By selling your soul."

A sternness filled Vanity's eyes, letting her eyelashes curl against her skin. She stepped closer to her charge, making sure she did not touch the Dancer. "I require no beat to fill my heart or to grant me power."

"My heart is my beat," the Dancer said.

The words hung in the air. Vanity had been ordered to find at least one Dancer and convert her. If one Dancer could become a believer, then the population would fall in line.

"My soul," the Dancer said, "is my power."

"It powers us all," Vanity said, relaxing her expression. "The soul is His gift to us all." She turned upward, looking through the skylight. Her eyes strained at the sight of her constantly gleaming god.

"If you believe in the sun so much, why do you squint your eyes?"

"Do not squint when you look upon our God," the Imperia said. "He is Helio-Asura, our maker, our creator." The statuesque woman's smile curled upward with sexual intent. "He is our everything."

Atsuko kept her head aimed up, but her eyes struggled to stay open. The warmth beat into her skin, clawing under the muscles that held her face together..

"Praise Him, girl."

Again, Atsuko recited the prayer. "Praise to Helio-Asura, our god and creator--"

The Imperia slapped Atsuko off the kneeler. Burning lines of moisture cut into Atsuko's cheek. A droplet fell from the tip of the Imperia's talons.

"You need conviction, adoration, and poise."

Drawing in a deep breath, Atsuko turned up at her mistress. "I said the words--"

The Imperia struck again, this time from the opposite side. "I would make you a queen among men, a goddess subservient only to me and to our God." She leaned down, lifting Atsuko's chin with a fingertip. "You must set aside all that you were. Cast it away and never look back."

For a moment, Atsuko looked up, breathing through her mouth. A tear threatened to flee from her left eye. "You've made me beautiful, so I want to do this. Tell me what you need from me and I'll give it to you."

The Imperia shoved Atsuko to the floor and stepped back. "Need? Nothing. I want everything from you. I have yet to see it."

Snapping her hand shut, the Imperia pulled her magic away from Atsuko. The strength of Atsuko's muscles faded, especially on the left side of her face. Collapsing to the stone floor, Atsuko pawed at the surface, chasing what the Imperia had given--and taken away.

Feebly, one word fell from Atsuko's lips. "Please..."

"Begging has never worked on me, child. Perhaps our God will be kind enough to burst you into flames and melt the rest of you away."

Atsuko whimpered. "No..."

The Imperia backhanded Atsuko before shoving the tips of five talons into Atsuko's neck. "Only through conviction can we ever rise. Give away that hidden core. Or listen to yourself whimper. Which do you think serves Helio-Asura more?"

Each tip sank deeper, though none struck Atsuko's windpipe or blood vessels. The tips drifted closer, drawing Atsuko toward action and attack or pain and torment.

Deformed again, Atsuko pulled back. Her eyes glared up at the Imperia but did not challenge the statuesque woman. Instead, Atsuko looked into the scorching light above, spreading her arms while her vision strained. "Praise to Helio-Asura." Atsuko drew in a deep breath. "Praise to our God and Creator."

She felt the words pulling at her neck even after speaking them. Her volume had risen, even though she still felt the wet lines cut into her face. "Praise the Death He Brings."

The Imperia nodded, her talons clattering as she flexed each finger. "Did you feel it, girl? The power of our God?"

Practically gasping, Atsuko said, "Yes." Something had pushed her, not pain, not even a survival instinct.

"Why did you choose pain?"

"It's always hurt." Atsuko kept looking up, focusing on the constant point of light overhead. "It's how I was made."

"Then I shall give you another gift." The Imperia thrust her index finger at Atsuko's chest. The elongated black tip stabbed deep into the healing heart. "Pray."

Without hesitation, Astuko turned her praise of the sun into a mantra. No tears escaped her as she spoke, though lightning struck from inside. A charge flashed through her throat, then pushed her face. The same force swelled her chest and hips, pulling on her limbs. Her senses wanted to scream, but the words kept rolling from her lips, over and again.

She stopped only when the words could not take shape. Panting pulled at her lungs and mouth.A buzzing flowed through her abdomen, surging where her senses met.

The Imperia pulled away, smiling too much with one side of her mouth. She moved a tall mirror forward. "I think you are much more than what you were, don't you think?"

Looking into the mirror, Atsuko saw her face and body. Everything about her had been perfected, almost to the level of the Imperia herself. There were no wounds in her body, no cuts on her face. "Yes, Imperia."

"When you open yourself to our God, He will restore your beauty. It will always hurt, but now you know the gift I have given you."

A satisfied grin formed in Atsuko's reflection. "I loved it."

With a laugh, the Imperia nodded. "I knew you were smarter than you let on."

"One cannot stare at God forever," Vanity said after a long pause.

The Dancer lifted an eyebrow, frowning from her web of restraints. "I don't buy it. You're quiet for that long and the best you can jab at me is some platitude one of the guards already gave me."

"Anyone can give a true answer."

"But if you're trying to convince me, you're blowing it."

Vanity reached for the straps around the Dancer's left arm. Touching the tight leather, Vanity knew that her own captivity had been to placate the guards. Her freedom was always in place. The Imperia knew every possible application of power and strength.

Vanity lowered her hand.

"Not going to let me go after all?" The Dancer snorted. "Just another pretty face to charm mayors into signing over their cities."

The tone of the Dancer's voice curled into Vanity's bones. Every scolding syllable sank deep. Vanity heard the tone before, striking at anyone who spoke at her.

That was Atsuko. That was the girl with the melted face. Born with disgust and disfigurement.

She was Vanity, not some pathetic thing.

Vanity pressed her fingers around the handle of her blade, sweeping it free from its sheath. The edge peeled through a layer of leather before rain poured over Vanity's face and pure white silks.

The Dancer gagged, her throat turned into a spraying fountain.

Vanity stared into the Dancer's pale violet eyes, watching the spark fade. One of the mages should have been summoned to fuel themselves with the fading death. Instead, Vanity watched and waited, letting the Dancer fade into nothing.

Jes pulled the Dancer's body out of the restraints, dragging her from the chamber, likely for meat curing. The other corpse slid out with another spearman's help.

Vanity did not look. Her thoughts stayed on the leather straps that kept the Dancer from releasing the forbidden rhythm. Vanity's fingers tightened around her blade, though she hadn't wiped away the blood.

There was more to Vanity than pleasing mayors and slashing throats. She turned to the mirror, looking at her reflection. Vanity's gaze locked not on the sweeping bands of red hair, but the random dots scattered over her silks.

Her knuckles popped from squeezing so hard. A knot of fire lingered between the bones of her index finger.

Vanity did not look up and speak her prayer. Instead, she stayed with her pain, watching the largest drop of blood creep down the side of her face.

Jes tapped on the chamber door and took a step inside. Lowering himself to one knee, he said, "Illumina, the Mayor of Mo-no has just arrived. Shall I send him in?"

"No," Vanity said. "I will see to him shortly. Tell him I have pleasant news regarding the rebel Dancer."

Clasping, his chest with a fist, Jes said, "Yes, Illumina," and backed out of the chamber.

With the spearman gone, Vanity looked at her reflection before preparing herself. She pressed her fingers to the left side of her face. In a whisper, she spoke her name. "Atsuko."

UNTITLED TRADITIONAL WORK CHANT

I see the sky
Curving up from me
I see the sky
Curving up from me

Climb up that line
Looped around on me
Climb up that line
Looped around on me

If I have to climb
Let me rise free
If I have to climb
Let me rise free

This traditional work chant has been used across many continental regions. A lead caller will sing each line while the chorus repeats the line before the caller continues to the next line. At the end of the third passage, the caller can loop back to the beginning to start the sequence once more.

In some areas, especially those liberated by the Order of the Turnip, the chorus with create an asynchronous harmony.

TEARS OF ICE

Tharkus sat upon the Ivory Throne watching as the women danced for him. A cup of mead lingered in his grasp. He propped his head against his fist, still clad in layers of armor.

Overhead, accents of sunlight washed over the earthen ceiling. Drums and strings pulsed behind Tharkus, but he remained numb to the beat. Not even the sway of scantily bodies could stimulate him.

"Go." Tharkus gave commands, he didn't speak in soft tones. Yet the women did not hear him. Batting his fingers away, Tharkus stared at the jagged threads of light.

The music drifted away. The women scampered away from the Ivory Throne. For gales, Tharkus continued to stare, swept away by darkness and silence.

A sultry voice drifted out of the shadows. "Mighty Tharkus, warlord of ice. I call to you."

Below the dais, a woman with piled red hair knelt with her head to the floor. A transparent cape drifted over her shoulders, flaring out like a pair of wings.

"Leave, Asurian. I'm not in the mood."

The woman lifted her head. A tiara of sculpted dragon bone sat above a wave of crimson bangs. Her full ruby lips tilted in a smirk. "If you think I have come to conquer, you are wrong."

Tharkus lifted the spear laying beside his throne.

Lifting her hands, the Asurian. "Peace, Mighty Tharkus. I haven't come for the glory of Asuria." She glanced up at the high ceiling and the muted rays of sunlight.

Tharkus tightened his grip. He could spill the woman's blood in an instant, but it would only satisfy her. The fanatics loved death, even if it was their own.

"Talk."

Even as she lowered her arms, the Asurian's smirk did not fade. "Thank you for sparing my life."

"For now." Tharkus slipped back into the Ivory Throne, tapping his spear against the dense armrest. He scowled.

"I want to solidify your rule. Perhaps expand it."

"An Asurian trying to become an Illumina." Tharkus shook his head. "I heard the Mayor of Mo-no announced his betrothal before his army marched on the Ash Coasts wearing Asurian colors."

The smirk straightened. "I am no longer an Illumina."

Tharkus stood, kicking the woman onto her back. Laughing, he pushed his spear against her throat. "Perhaps Sorcha Kagatsu will thank me for killing her rival."

Before Tharkus could pierce the woman's skin, she screeched. "I renounced them!"

He pulled his spear back. "Them?"

The Asurian breathed deep. "Asuria. The Imperia. Helio-Asura."

Tharkus laughed again and sat, leaving the spear across his lap. "Kagatsu would have your tongue for that, even if it was a joke." He tapped his fingers on the spear shaft. "Let's have it. No lead-up. Tell me why you're here."

The woman gave a light smirk. "The Frozen Crown. It's said to men and magic alike."

"It's in a tomb full of frozen corpses."

"What if I knew a way around that?"

Tharkus tilted his hand dismissively. "It wouldn't matter. You'd be dead before you got there."

The Asurian's mouth shifted into a full smile. "You could do it with the right pyromancy."

Of all the treasures Tharkus had taken, he told no one of the legacy of the Ash Coasts. Most people, if they were to see the brand, would think nothing of it. Yet this woman knew Tharkus had it. Or at least suspected.

"There are no pyromancers," Tharkus said. "Your former mistress wiped them out."

"That's funny. I met a pyromancer on my way here." The Asurian shrugged and relaxed. "She told me of a few pyromancies that could deal with dense ice."

Shaking his head, Tharkus pressed a finger against his brow. "A wayward traveler gave you the clue you needed? Your story is getting thin."

If she proved worth the effort, Tharkus was sure he would keep the Asurian around. A rogue Asurian could surely be trained.

"I was searching for any clue to reach the Frozen Crown. When I met this pyromancer, I was as skeptical as you are now."

"How did she convince you?"

The Asurian traced her finger on the floor in an angular pattern. Tharkus widened his eyes when he realized the familiar pattern.

"You've seen the brand, Mighty Tharkus. This is the pattern it burns into flesh—the same pattern that grants power over fire." The Asurian straightened her posture, resting her hands against her abdomen. "I need you to use the brand on me, then I can reach the Crown."

Tharkus snorted. "What do I get for this?"

The Asurian loosened her thin hood and cloak, making her piled crimson hair even more visible. "I will give you allegiance and affection."

Nodding, Tharkus knew he could take either offering whenever he liked. The Asurian only needed to make it worth his trouble.

The Asurian shifted so she sat rather than knelt. "You can conquer anything you like. Have you ever considered what you would gain from a worthy queen? Any Illumina could fit in with those other girls. Have you ever wondered what it would be like to have something more?"

Tharkus lifted his brow. "How could an Illumina ever be worthy?"

"I'm not—"

"I know what you said." Tharkus let his volume rise as he leaned closer. "Stop being vague and tell me why I shouldn't have you flogged?" He sighed at his choice of words. A flogging could never scar an Illumina.

A small tremor parted the Asurian's lips. Her eyes snapped down before daring to gaze up with her answer. "With the crown, I could bear both fire and ice. As your queen, you could present me as you wish. Who could possibly stand against a man who had taken an Illumina's loyalty from Asuria itself?"

Tharkus shook his head. "I have nothing to enforce that loyalty."

The woman stood while her eyes stayed fixed on Tharkus. "I know you have the pyromantic brand. If I wasn't being honest with you, I would have come with a swarm of dragons and legions of soldiers." She spread her arms and turned in a circle. "I came here alone. I don't want to see your vaults, I only want you to use one of your treasures."

"Damn. That actually makes sense. Wait here." Tharkus marched out huffing.

The Ash Coasts had burned so the Imperia could gain power over fire—and she'd failed. No Illumina would be allowed to succeed in her place.

Gales drifted in and out of the deepest cave lying far beneath the Ivory Throne. Tharkus could see his breath clinging to the air around him. Row upon row of tools and trophies sat under three elevated beacons. Even with the masses of flame, Tharkus felt closer to the realms of demons than the radiance of the sun.

Tharkus grumbled as he pulled aside another clump of metal. A dragon rider's pike, a free mage's staff, and several beacons from fallen Mo-no—but no brand.

Groaning, he shut his eyes and tossed the rods aside.

"Mighty Tharkus cannot be so easily defeated." The Asurian took several steps into the vault, her hips slithering back and forth over some invisible line. A cloud of frozen air billowed from her full lips, even as she still wore an Illumina's open costume. "If you like, I can help. My instructors always thought my focus was untainted."

Tharkus closed his fists. "What do you know, woman?" He shook his head. "I don't know why I'm doing this for you. I don't even—"

"Purity."

"What?" Intensity raged through Tharkus's voice, enough to keep his echo at the same general volume.

The Asurian maintained her composure, even as she stood demurely. "Purity is my name." She sighed, giving a bounce to her chest. "If you would prefer I had a different name—"

"You deal with your own name. I've always been Tharkus." He shoved his hand into a cluster of bone-bladed weapons. They weren't too good for an Asurian, even if she had defected. "I know who I am. Do you know who you are?"

Purity smiled and minced forward again. She rubbed the palm of her right hand before opening it to Tharkus. "Your queen. Once you make me a pyromancer."

"I have to find the damned thing first."

"Isn't that it?" Purity tilted her head toward the cluster of weapons.

Close to Tharkus's knuckles, a blackened length of metal as tall as a child stood out. Warmth radiated from the protective handle before Tharkus locked his hand around it. He pulled the rod loose from the pile just as heat ripped into his elbow. "It's still warm."

Purity moved close, leaning toward the emblemed end. Her mouth hung open and her eyes stopped blinking.

"Fantastic coincidence," Tharkus said. The beacons were too high to heat anything on the floor. "How does this work?"

Purity twitched as she hopped out of her demeanor. "We need the hottest fire you have. There need to be open flames, coals aren't enough."

The host of Tharkus's guards slept in the halls, leaving every passage unchecked. Saliva swirled inside his mouth as he prodded one of his prone followers.

"Don't chastise them too much." Purity pulled the translucent cape around her body and clasped her abdomen. "Much of this is my doing." Slender fingers pressed against a token embedded under her left ear. Four growing arcs filled the circle. "I've been making my way here for some time."

"Gages in your ears, a ring in your nose, and a mark on your head. You're a glutton for it."

"Everyone makes themselves better. This is my path."

"If you like."

They stepped into the open air, letting the sun hammer their eyes as it washed over Winter's Tusk. Tharkus didn't alter his flesh to prove his worth. He scoured the fang of an ancient demon, forging a castle around the Ivory Throne. Around the Tusk, barracks held the legions that had pledged themselves. More and more of his followers brought their families into his protection.

Perhaps Purity knew this was the moment she could make herself a queen. The woman's tenacity bordered disrespect, but she always returned to deference.

At the start of the street leading to Winter's Tusk, a wide pit rolled with flames, a beacon to endure any weather. The guardians all slept next to their charge, appearing as the laziest sentries.

Tharkus rested the brand against his shoulder. "You did all this?"

"When the wind wills it. My mark is strong, but it's a slave to the weather."

"A bad gale will strip you of your power."

"It is only one power." Purity extended her right hand. "There are others."

Tharkus grabbed Purity's neck with his free hand. His might thrust her close to the flames. He pushed down, forcing her body to collapse on the stone road.

She squealed. "You only have to—"

"Command you?" Tharkus struck Purity's back with his knee until she lay flat. "You don't understand what it means to serve me." He thrust the brand into the beacon.

Purity's limbs and flesh reflexively wriggled. "T-train me."

"Train? I'm not some haughty Imperia impressing everyone with mass suicide. This is the real world, the cold world. People live here and it hurts. But we live."

Purity breathed slower, turning her hand over. "I am yours to do with as you like. Brand me and I will treat it as proof…" She paused and her voice sank. "You own me."

"We shall see." Tharkus drew the gleaming brand and plunged it into Purity's hand. Her scream roused the sleeping bodies.

Along with five of his followers, Tharkus rode through snow drifts. His grip on his mount's antlers remained steady. His men tended to jerk when they rode, enraging the byaks.

Purity sat atop the broad furred beast, leaving her arms crossed. Steam billowed around the woman, especially the palm of her right hand.

The man riding on the opposite side of Tharkus laughed. "She looks sad, your little pyromancer. All warm and all alone."

Purity glanced at the man with saturated eyes.

"There's no need for that, Jerid. Purity knows her place now." Tharkus rode closer, gripping Purity's piled locks. "She had a little pride before, but that's gone now."

She stroked Tharkus's arm and kissed his knuckles. "Purged." Purity's smile rose, weaker than it had been.

"When we finish, we might make a Coldstone of you yet." Tharkus let go, nudging his byak toward a narrow angle of rock thrusting out of the snow.

"That's the lower Tusk," Jerid said. "Nothing there but molten rock and a slab of ice no one can touch." Jerid and the others picked up their pace.

Purity kept to her deliberate pace.

Tharkus shook his head as he looked back. "I must have broken you."

Purity rode onward with the others.

Charred arms jutted out of the cave walls. Broken statues of permafrost cried in agony. More fractured bodies filled the passage approaching the Frozen Crown.

It had never been a matter of fire. Some of the bodies still gripped intact torches.

"Wait a moment." Purity walked ahead of the others. Gingerly, she shut her eyes and reached into the dark. Where there had been shadows, light surged.

Dozens of hands blazed with fire. More ignited as Purity walked into the tunnel.

Jerid looked up and down the tunnel. "Why do only some of the corpses glow?"

"They are pyromancers," Purity said. "The ones who failed."

Tharkus planted his spear with one hand and grabbed Purity's shoulder with the other. "No one's trained you. This isn't going to work."

Purity shrugged. "You still have the brand. If I fail, I'll be dead." Her mass swept toward Tharkus, pressing a firm kiss into his lips. "If I fail, I was never worthy of you."

More corpses lit, bursting into flame. At the heart of the tunnel, a column of glistening ice sealed an angular crown. Petrified skeletons reached out of the floor, unable to touch their prize.

Purity walked down the tunnel, circling the column twice. "There are three locks holding the crown in place. First, is the bond of blood. Jerid, sweetie, your tongue sickens me."

"Worry about the crown," Tharkus said.

Tharkus's followers surrounded Jerid, bracing him. One jerked the man's mouth open.

Tharkus spun his spear into attack position. "What is this?"

"Don't worry, Mighty Tharkus. I have to keep your head clear."

A wet gargle echoed through the cave. One of the men walked downward with a dark clump of flesh.

"Second is the reluctant gift." Purity reached toward the man. "Come to me."

Tharkus hurled his spear down the tunnel.

The brand on Purity's hand ignited, burning the spear to ash.

While staring at his bare hands, the Coldstones—including Jerid—shoved Tharkus aside. Ice gripped their arms and legs, slowing their descent. Each step flinched, turning more rigid.

"What is this?"

Purity lifted a single finger toward Tharkus before approaching his followers. She used the dark clump to draw a ring on the column.

Inside, the Frozen Crown sparkled.

"The third lock is the simplest. A gentle affectation." Purity kissed the center of the ring. When she pulled back, part of the column grew dark and fell away like sludge.

Purity tossed the clump aside and clapped. Her cheeks became flush with warmth. "Perfect." She slashed her hand at the followers, setting them all on fire.

"You killed my men."

"You've spent lives on this before, I'm sure." Purity jerked the Asurian tiara from her head, letting the attached cape blow away from her. After a long exhale, she reached into the column with both hands.

When Purity eased out the Frozen Crown, Tharkus charged.

Whips of permafrost snapped out of the wall, coiling around Tharkus. He ripped away from one, but two more shot out. A chill rippled through Tharkus. He tightened the tension between his teeth, dragging his arms up. More icy slush warped around his limbs, tickled a path over his torso and spine.

Purity traced her fingers over the Frozen Crown, sighing from her core. "Oh, Tharkus, it's exquisite."

He grunted, jerking at the growing womb of ice.

With a lick of her lips, Purity's skin grew pale. She stopped blinking, looking only at the Crown and the brand seared into her palm. "It's fitting that you still fight. You're right that the Imperia comes for everyone. I could never stand up to her." Her expression cooled, but her smile remained. "You couldn't either. I did sneak into your throne room without any interference."

Tharkus growled, his jaw opening enough to deliver him enough force to move.

Purity flicked a finger, spewing flames into Tharkus's path. Fire slapped him back into the hardening mass.

Set deeper into the mass of ash and crystal, Tharkus roared again. His face flushed with heat, even as his armor baked into the mountain core.

"Purity was a name impressed on me, all because the Imper—" Purity spat, then grinned. "Because Sorcha Kagatsu wanted me to be her toy. I'm done with all that now. Watch Tharkus. Take what you see to that bitch's god and teach him to fear." She touched the layers of dragon weave bound to her Asurian office, setting them ablaze.

Once every article of her clothing glistened with impossible flame, Purity held the Frozen Crown overhead with both hands. "Ice and fire are bound to me, enslaving me as I will enslave all your men. Let the smoke take Purity from my body and harden my power." Spirals of ice drifted around the woman, sparing her skin the burden of blistering in heat. Moisture poured out of her eyes, drenching her cheeks. "I proclaim myself Heika Kori, Goddess of the Elements."

"No matter your name," Tharkus said, "I will rip away your tongue and make you watch as I carve steaks from your hide."

The Frozen Crown pressed against Hekia Kori's forehead as she giggled. Icy dust chilled her skin, fusing the Crown to her skull. Her eyes burst with fire, freezing into onyx orbs a moment later. Cold bleached her lips a deep purple, bordering close to blue. A trail of frozen white patterned her lower lip just as she ran her fingers through her hair. Ice bleached the strands framing her face. Fire crisped the locks coiled above her Crown.

Sheets of soot froze around the woman's body, fanning in a crest around her neck and draping her in a deadly winter's gown. The air around her nose and mouth froze with her every breath.

Heika Kori leaned close to Tharkus, keeping the smile Purity wore before the Ivory Throne. "I could free you now that I'm whole. All you have to do is say my name, praise and worship me—then you can live. What do you think?"

"No goddess would ever need to ask my opinion."

"True. Good thing I already knew it."

Heika Kori glided away from Tharkus. A dismissive tilt of her hand buried him in flames an instant before the world froze around him.

Tharkus no longer spoke. The rest of his eternal life was spent screaming.

When the Coldstones found Tharkus seasons later, screaming echoed in their ears.

By then, they'd already pledged themselves to Heika Kori.

WHEN THE SUN FELL

One climbed out
Not a man
Not a beast
He broke the shard
Bits scattered afar

Hammer down
Clang! Clang!
Crack away
Clang! Clang!

Cold and fright
Shadows in delight
One climbed out
Shed a tear
Made it right

Hammer down
Clang! Clang!
Crack away
Clang! Clang!

Blade, Flame, and Ray
Towers rose
Monuments high
Cities floated
Shy of the sky

Hammer down
Clang! Clang!
Crack away
Clang! Clang!

Another reached down
Not a man
Not a beast
Stole the hero
For making peace

Hammer down
No clang, no clang
Anvil cold
Away we stay

A Town with No Water

No matter how she moved her mouth, Lora's lips still cracked from the heat. The eternal sun reflected off the mirror sheen of the desert. Rather than cover her brow, she kept her throbbing eyes shut.

Her companion's hollow voice broke the silence. "We should get you a hood."

"I'm fine." No matter how many seasons they'd traveled together, Lora still scowled when Carson tried to protect her. She might have grown to adulthood in his care, but he always hovered nearby, ready to strike.

The solemn protective voice rumbled from under the dusty black hood concealing his head and face. "How's your water?"

Lora reached between her coat and her spine and grabbed the leather bottle hooked to her belt. Nothing moved inside. She shook her head.

The knight's black hood nodded. Lora rarely saw Carson's face, a fact she was sometimes grateful for. Time stopped for no one, not even the dead. "We'll stop at Lai Cross. It's close to the First River."

No matter how hot the winds blew or how many clouds failed to obscure the sun, water remained essential. Even if she swam in the First River, Lora's right hand would remain a charred fist. Once her smoky fingers hadn't been flexible ash.

Pyre lived up to its name in its final moments. As the capital of the Ash Coasts, Pyre offered faith, flames, and prosperity to its people and the surrounding region.

As a young girl, Lora didn't move as pure white buildings exploded. People outside screamed in every direction. Shrill dragon cries tore through the air, making Lora's shoulders shake. The prior and his disciples ran through the temple carrying spears and knives along with their incense-drenched flames. Lora's father, the King of Xeryt, followed them for a moment, then looked at Lora.

He snatched her into his blanketed arms. "Come on. We have to hurry."

Lora would have run by her father's side, but he ran so fast. Her fingers clamped around the hand-sized patch of white knitting. It was the best she'd ever done with one of the feminine arts. Even though it only had the Crest of Xeryt, Lora had trimmed her own hair to make the gold lining.

When they reached the end of the chiseled cavern hall, two small pits of lava bubbled in the back of the ritual chamber. A narrow diamond-shaped platform held up a black and yellow shrine of solid magma. She'd never been inside the Altar of the Burning Hand as part of any ritual. Only disciples and her parents even entered such a sacred place.

Lora's father put her down next to the shrine. Worn spots pushed into the platform where others had knelt many times before. "Lora, can you be brave for me?"

She nodded. Her father was always the smartest, nicest person. If he wanted her to be brave, she could be brave.

Lora's mother ran inside a moment later, carrying Lora's younger brother, Laren. "What are you waiting for?" Mother asked. "We need to give them both the hand."

Constant walking strained the young woman's knees. The pale, boxy shapes of simple huts drew into focus ahead of her. Beside the desolate town was a shallow valley desperate to remember moisture. "I thought we were heading for the First River."

"We have been." Carson took a compass from his belt and held it so the wind could move through the lower vents. The needle aligned itself with the strongest currents. "This is Lai Cross."

"Then where is the river?" Lai Cross was affiliated with Carson's homeland, the most elusive realm people sometimes visited. Drought was impossible for a minor waypoint on the path to Shabra-Lai. Lora flexed her right hand at the ruined clay watchtower at the edge of the town. "Where is the bloody river?"

Carson stepped closer, closing his hand over the young woman's extended wrist. "Calm down."

Flames sprang between Carson's gloved fingers. Trails of smoke smoldered from where he held her exposed wrist. Lora screamed. She'd burned her life away without realizing it. Shaking her head, the flames died from her hand, retreating to her charcoal flesh.

Lora marched away in grief after Carson let go of her. A slender thread of pain crept up her arm, rising higher than the crusted ash along her forearm. It would take several seasons for the mark of her power to claim her elbow. Someday, it might even reach her shoulder. Only the Elder Prior lived long enough for the Burning to cover more than his arm and take the last spark of his life.

Father put Lora's right hand on the altar, sliding her small fingers into several finger-shaped grooves. The indentation was too big for her hand, since children couldn't gain the Burning Hand. Lora was at least fifteen seasons away from coming into her maturity. How did her parents expect her to take on the Burning Hand?

Laren seemed just as confused. Mother plunged the Burning Spike in the brazier between the two beds of lava. The narrow diamond design of the platform repeated itself in the Burning Spike. Her mother's ritual tool extended to a narrow point glowing white hot after exiting the lava.

Lora didn't know fighting. She spent her time trying to knit.

"Stay still, sweetheart." Father stroked the side of Lora's face with his right hand. Even though he wore black gloves, Father's hand was a sinewy mass of burned flesh and scorched bones. It still moved with the same agility and function as his left hand, though he made sure never to touch anyone with the bare ashes.

Voices cried out from a distant hallway before trailing off. Disciples shouted. A few tossed aside their outer robes.

"Father." Lora looked up with trembling eyes. "What's happening?"

"The Asurians have come." His lips strained as he scowled at the sky. When he met Lora's gaze, his grip on her hand tightened. "Hold still."

Cracked stone huts with thatched roofs spread out in front of Lora. Streets with simple yellow-brown bricks crept through the town. Sedentary cooking pits lingered near the larger huts, while bare hitching posts marked where beasts of burden had once visited. A round brick monolith anchored the center of the town. Even without a roof, thick leather flaps closed the structure off from the rest of the town.

Wary of what might hide inside the monolith, Lora drew both of her short swords. The narrow blades caught the light, though swirling burn marks covered the weapon in her right hand. She held her pristine sword ahead of her, while keeping the burned blade up and ready to strike. Only then did she ease the flap aside and step inside.

Discarded pots lay all around Lora. Cracked flakes of eroded pottery fell along the modest ring of bricks at the heart of the monolith. A crank hung over a shadowed well, lowering a forgotten rope into the earthen abyss. Lora sheathed her blades and turned the crank a few times. The smell of rotten fish and starving maggots clawed into the air.

She ran outside, gagging as she fell to her knees. Carson's thunderous steps raced toward her.

The white-hot blade was beyond intimidating. It was wider than a finger. Sharp, threatening. Its approach hurt as much as the stabbing pain that followed. The Prior coached her breathing, but all little Lora knew was that the blade hurt. Terror shook her arm. If she pulled away, it might stop hurting.

Father squeezed her elbow and clamped down on her wrist. He leaned over her, pushing his weight down like a fearless anchor.

Lora's hand shook in reflexive defiance. The metal emblem of Xeryt anchored her into compliance. The Brand didn't need any readjustment. Flame ejected from the contact, screaming for power to flood into the girl's hand.

Tender meat cooked around the impact. Tears rolled away from Lora as unwanted hunger stirred her stomach. She screamed, unable to make out the ritual words Father said. Chanting disciples didn't break the rising agony.

The twin lava pools took on a brighter luster, daring Lora to imagine a steaming bath. She heard the old stories about how Xeryt wanted all of a person's flesh. If she could get away from the Burning.

"Lora." Mother's voice billowed behind her right ear. "Purge the fire from your hand. Push it away from your palm and fingers. Hold your hand toward a lava pool and let the ember go free."

The Burning Brand tore upward, freeing Lora's hand. Ashy crust cracked as she lifted her right arm. Flames and smoke flared along the edges of the smoking emblem of Xeryt burned into her hand.

The slight gap in her Lora's palm made a fine target. Her wrist pushed forward, releasing a thin stream of fire. Each flaming pop drifted into the open, leaving her fingers cooler than ever before. She pushed again, forcing more cold fire away from her hand.

Lora stepped backward. Her right hand disgusted her more than some forced healthy meal. But it moved normally.

A gale rushed above Lora's head, tickling hair back and forth over her brow. Almost none of the diseased smell lingered in the breeze. The cleaner environment let Lora rest on a wooden dock supported by stone pillars. Beneath her, the shallow valley grew darker at lower depths.

She glanced at the lowest part of the valley peeking through the charred slit in her right hand. Every flame made the hole widen, though not enough to cut off her sensations.

More cracks formed on her lips. Her tongue was a lump of leather. Her single-sleeved studded leather coat dragged her shoulders downward. Breathing made her chest plate ease upward for only an instant before she exhaled.

"You're tired." Carson's voice rose with a somber fact. His dutiful compulsion to defend her rose from a drive neither of them understood.

She couldn't waste energy just to look at him. "I am. What's your plan?"

"You need water." Carson never let Lora use him to carry gear. Still, his gravel voice rumbled with compassion.

For seasons, Lora begged him to carry more water. She bought an extra water skin when she realized he'd never agree. It didn't stop his concern or hinder his protective instincts. It never kept him front standing guard when Lora slept. "Do you have a plan?"

"We could look to see if there's a dam."

Lora faced the shallow valley long enough to take a few breaths. The darkest rocks in the valley looked like they'd been mud only a few gales earlier. "There will be."

"How do you know?"

Carson had inserted one of his damned survival lessons into her misery.

"The valley was recently mud here. Darker stones and soil mean water saturation. The water might be blocked on the surface, but the water table is intact. Aside from the well."

Carson's armor clanked as he sat next to Lora. She glimpsed the calcified rot that memorialized his nose. He scratched his scraggly beard for a moment, then lowered his head. His hood slipped forward, throwing more shadows onto his face. "I never wanted to fail your father."

"They're dead." If Lora had the strength for rage, she would have struck the knight. If she had any excess water, she might have cried in her repressed rage. "I'm sure my brother is too."

Carson's voice burst like a backfiring cannon. "You don't know that."

"No." Unresolved grief hardened her voice. "I don't."

Pain shifted from hyperintensity to inconsistent prickling in Lora's hand. More shouting erupted from the hallways. Foreign soldiers wearing black and red sashes clashed with the disciples outside of the ritual chamber. The attackers were lean with stringy muscles, bronzed skin, and inconsistent bits of armor. Angular blades smeared with blood hung from their hands like hungry talons.

Mother pushed Laren deeper into the chamber and spun on the tips of her toes. She opened her right hand and screamed at the intruders. Flames roared out, enveloping any Asurians who made it past the disciples. When the flames stopped, the intruders had turned to embers, kindling several man-shaped torches.

"We don't have time to finish." Father carried the Brand away from Lora, holding the hot, bladed end away from his face and body. Kneeling in front of Laren, Father said, "Hold this for me."

Laren reached up with small, shaky hands, taking the brand. When Father let go, Laren stumbled, barely clinging to his charge.

Lora was a big girl. Her right hand hurt, but she was strong enough to hold a metal stick. "I can carry it."

Father's large hand fell on Lora's shoulder. "No." He'd never been so quiet that Lora understood how much he hurt. "You have to go another way. If you stay together, it will be easier for them to find you."

"Asurians use everything." The understanding glided beneath Lora's rancid breath.

Carson's head lifted. "What was that?"

"The Asurians aren't wasteful. If they can't use something, they destroy it."

Carson faced the town. "Everything is still here."

"They destroyed the Ash Coasts in fifty gales. They'd erase this town in two." Lora got up from the abandoned dock, walking back toward the brick huts. "Why didn't they?"

"They wanted something."

"No." Lora stepped off the dock, pacing herself so Carson could catch up. "They already took what they wanted."

Carson's armor kept him at mortal speeds. "They haven't destroyed the town yet."

"You always say Asurians don't tolerate laziness."

Carson his neck and back. A wet click echoed his adjusting joints. "What are you thinking?"

"There are Asurians upriver from here. They aren't far, because someone had to poison that well."

"You think they're after the water."

Lora shook her head. "No. They'd have killed everyone and taken the town if they only wanted water. I think they're after the townsfolk."

Father pulled Lora by the arm. Salty tears ran over her cheeks. Mother dragged Laren in the opposite direction without looking back.

"Where are we going?" Lora screamed. Her eyes were too wide to weep, too frantic to blink. "Where are we going!"

Father charged onward, certain of his unspoken destination. "You need someone to protect you."

"Mother and Laren can protect us." The girl jerked against her father's grip, unable to break loose. "We can protect them."

"Your mother and I have to stay and fight." The floor tiles shook free of their plaster. A celebratory banner whipped free from the wall. Dust fell from the ceiling. Pebbles echoed all around them. "Xeryt will break if she and I don't stay and fight."

Lora held up her right hand. "I can fight too. Let me help you."

"You have to escape. I gave you the Burning Hand so Xeryt will survive, even if the Ash Coasts don't."

"We can fight them." Fearful tears of rage flowed from Lora's eyes, paralleling the two fonts of lava she'd just visited. Father's mouth soured when he looked in her eyes. A cloud of sadness clung to the lines in his face.

Five priests ran past, cradling their right arms. A sixth priest followed them with a curved, blood-stained knife and a woven green bag with a blackened sunburst.

"You are too young to fight them," Father said. "But we found someone who will teach you."

Carson led the way, cautious of Asurian death magic. His armor clanked and scraped with every step. He kept a battered round shield mounted on his back. Underneath, an aged sword hung against his spine. His hood remained up, since he hated exposing himself to the eternal sun. Lora had only seen the ruination of his exposed head on a handful of occasions during their shared exile.

They ventured upriver, leaving the vacated town behind them. Lora didn't look back. She'd seen enough homes drift up the horizon before fading into the distance behind her. Sometimes because she fled, sometimes because she didn't care to stay in one place for long.

Dryness chewed at her lips. Barbs of pain pierced through the dull pain in her knees. She rubbed her right hand, massaging tension away from the Emblem of Xeryt.

Lora knew better than to ask her goddess for a drink. The only answer she ever got was silence. Lora didn't want to consider what might happen if a divine answer came.

Several catacombs pierced the lower coastline of the Ash Coasts. Black sand as powdery as fine snow stretched in a web of paths, broken only by fresh water crashing into the battered mountain holding the center of Xeryt intact. Desperate people ambled away from the city, constantly wary of explosions or the dragons that caused them. Only four constables escorted the travelers on the first steps of their mass journey.

A woman with the Crest of Xeryt tattooed on her forehead passed around a ceramic knife, helping the faithful sacrifice one hand each in desperate offering. The tattooed woman still had both of her hands, no matter how much the pool of discarded blood grew.

A hooded knight in reflective armor stood against a wall, watching the faithful pass. Every plate of the knight's armor was metal, something Lora had only heard tales about. Most tools and weapons were made of ceramic or thin stone shards. She couldn't see the knight's face, though the bearded part of his chin edged out from under the folds of his black hood.

When Lora stopped in front of the knight, his palm rested on a leather-wrapped knife handle.

The scene around Lora forced her to look into the knight's abyssal hood. "Are you going to cut off my hand?"

"No." The knight's voice was hollow, empty like he hadn't drunk anything for seasons.

Father leaned down, pulling Lora close to him. "This is Carson. He's a powerful knight from Shabra-Lai. If anyone asks, he's your uncle. If anyone asks you where you're from, tell them you're from Shabra-Lai. Can you remember that?"

Lora's eyes moistened as she shook her head. "I don't want to go."

Father frowned while his eyebrows rose with focused authority. "It's not safe for you here, Lora. Now, who is this knight?"

Lora sniffed and wiped at her nose with her left hand. "He's my uncle."

Carson looked down and asked, "Where are we from, Lora?"

"Shabra-Lai." She shifted away from them both.

A wounded smile formed on Father's face. "Good." He kissed Lora on the forehead. The sensation beamed with more love than the sun had light. When Father pulled away, an awful tremor shook through his entire body. "I love you, Lora."

Father turned and marched away. His steps were fast-paced, then grew quicker. He crashed into a couple of huddled women before fleeing even faster. As he dashed back into the city tunnels, Father's arm covered his face.

Lora didn't know that she should have kept him in sight. She didn't understand why he was running away from her. She was being sent away by herself, only having a stranger to keep her company.

Lora's feet ached from carrying on without hydration. Sunlight burned hotter than usual, an inferno rather than just a simple battering of endless heat into her skin. Her eyes drooped as she ambled behind Carson's constant pace.

As Lora walked, the grasses under her boots turned paler shades of brown. The highest threads of vegetation crumbled at the slightest amount of contact. A gale swept all around her, scattering dead plants into the next generation of dust.

Heavy grains of sand and skittering feet rustled behind Lora. Her eyes followed the path leading back to Lai Cross. Bumbling, wiry masses of fur trotted on and off the trail, all leaving the town behind them. A scent reminded Lora of the putrid well when the little scavengers dashed around her and Carson.

Even the smallest creatures fled Lai Cross. Desperation drove her. Hunger pushed the little bodies around Lora. The impulse within her calmed at the frayed possibility they all united to take revenge on the Asurians. Surviving their cruelty was one form of vengeance. Every endured breath, each refusal to kneel, all the minor denied conquests added up to something greater.

Hope pulsed through Lora's head, clotting her blood vessels. She stumbled off the imaginary line following Carson, turning upward.

Far above, the sun offered no glory, not even to the crazed masses pledged to kill everyone and everything.

A moment later, she heard her name and saw darkness.

As the underground tunnels led away from Pyre, a thick smoke lingered over everything. People fled, running inland toward the farms bloated with ripened egg beans, rather than risk being seen on boats in the open sea.

Inhuman roars exploded overhead. Lora looked back and saw a dragon spewing molten plasma over the temples. Thick clouds of smoke hid the creature, but everyone recognized the menace. A quartet of broad, sinewy wings raced into and out of view, screeching while sun worshipers prodded the beast. There was no way Father and Mother could fight a flying menace.

"They don't follow small groups of people." Carson tugged Lora's hand, guiding her to follow one of the scattered streams of people. "We'll get away and we'll be safe."

Lora didn't resist as they left the Ash Coasts behind. Every step they took moved them further from Father and Mother. Yet the dragon always swooped and screeched directly overhead.

"They're going to die." The words fell away from Lora's lower lip, crashing to the surface the dragon avoided.

"A lot of people already have."

The young girl wiped her eyes with the back of her free hand. "I don't want Father to die." Lora held her arm in front of her eyes. "Or Laren or Mother or the Abbott–"

Carson knelt in front of Lora. Small beads glistened inside his hood, the only sign of his eyes. He laid a hand on her shoulder, squeezing with strong, thin fingers. After a few panicked breaths from Lora, Carson spoke. "It's hard, but the Asurians can be fought. They can even be beaten. The people of Shabra-Lai even made them retreat."

She wiped her eyes again, just as the tears stopped. "Father's going to make them run away?"

"He might. Even if he survives, you may never see him again." Carson massaged her shoulder much as her father did. "I promised him I would protect you. As long as I'm with you, your father's hope for you endures."

Lora nodded, giving no further objection. Together, they left the Ash Coasts in the past.

A sharp bitterness filled Lora's mouth. Warm, thick goop made her gag. Her eyes opened as she sat up. Carson sat next to her, holding her by the shoulders. "Steady. You passed out for a bit."

Lora shook her head and blinked the daze from her eyes. "What happened?"

"You needed water. You still do." Carson lifted his foot, retrieving a furry scavenger trapped underneath. He grabbed the creature's head and twisted, tossing the small mass aside before passing the remains to Lora. "Drink."

She took the small, twitching body. Lora coiled her hands tight around the little beast, making sure it didn't escape. Coarse, prickly fur scratched at her fingers. After a deep breath, she raised the scavenger's neck to her lips and drank more of the hot goop.

Her taste buds begged to vomi. The stink of bile couldn't stir in Lora's nose. Thirst overtook her. She gulped down the small creature's blood. Lora took a deep breath and widened her eyes. As she tilted her head back, a few more drops landed in her mouth.

"Better?" Carson asked.

Lora flicked her tongue and nodded. With her vision stable again, she dropped the scavenger's body inside of her trail bag. Eventually, she would get hungry.

∞

After a season away from the Ash Coasts, Carson led Lora to a caravan. Together, they traveled toward Mono, a city where most religions were welcome. Keeping her right arm covered, the young girl enjoyed walking beside the mantorses dragging the wagons. Sometimes, their owners would let her touch each beast's smooth carapace, though her protector often eased her away.

"We have to be careful," he said. "We don't know who might be Asurian, or willing to take their money."

"Aren't they back home?"

"They're everywhere. They want to destroy the world. It's their religion."

"Like how Tyrex always fought Xyret?"

"Yes. They say their religion is the only truth."

"What about Mother and Father's temple? What about the other places where people pray?"

"They burned temples on Shabra-Lai before they went to the Ash Coasts. When they burn temples, they build new ones to honor their god and tell people how to pray."

"I'd just lie to them."

"They would kill you if they found out. Death makes them stronger."

Lora said nothing. Mantorses were better company than the thought of Asurian invaders.

Lora gulped down the blood of another scavenger while she walked. The taste still turned her nose with its thick bitterness, but she needed the strength. She needed more if she was going to fight Asurians. Even if the followers of death weren't nearby, Lora needed to rest, drink, and fill her bottle.

Carson pointed to a shadow at the visible edge of the rising horizon. "Three leagues ahead on the left."

Dropping the most recent scavenger into her bag, Lora covered her brow.

A claw-shaped stone fort of stone grasped for the sky beyond the shallow valley. A towering bridge connected the fort to a craggy rock incline on the opposite side of the former river. People moved outside of the lowest tower in the keep, shifting up and down a wooden framework. Two columns of fire on the periphery reached into the sky. Every stone finger released steam from its tip.

"What is that?"

Carson shook his head. "Red and black robes."

Lora scowled as possibilities became reality. "You have a plan?"

He held out a finger, tracing the lines of the claw-shaped fort in the distance. He pointed toward the bridge on the same side he and Lora stood on. "I'm going to stay on the right. I'll use that bridge to get across. Wait two gales, then rush through the valley. Sweep up the opposite side when you get under the bridge. If there's a dam, use it to meet me at the keep."

"I'm going to break down any dam I find."

Carson drew his sword, a blade of weathered steel that he laid over his right shoulder. The knight refused to trade his most favored tools and protection for a single drop of moisture. "I'll see you on the inside." His metal armor shifted and clanked as he charged into the distance.

"You're holding it too tight." Carson loomed close to Lora, studying her combative efforts from the safety of his oppressive hood.

Lora's first sword had been a narrow ceramic sword with a short grip. In a child's hands, it might as well weigh as much as the observant knight. Lora's small body hadn't been used to the strain.

She grunted and clamped her teeth together, desperate to keep her grip on the sword. "I can't lift it if I don't hold it this tight."

Emptiness rushed away from Carson. His crossed arms remained absolutely still as Lora kept huffing. "You're not strong enough yet."

Lora scowled. "Are you going to teach me or not?"

Carson nodded decisively. "I will. The first lesson is holding the weapon." He repositioned the sword where the blade lay on Lora's right shoulder. "Let gravity help you. You have to respect having something deadly in your hand."

She glanced at her gloved right hand. Even with a glove, the Burning Hand was a deadly weapon in itself. The slightest force of will would set anything on fire.

The Burning Hand could burn the world.

Both of Lora's narrow ceramic and bone swords pulled down toward the ground as she entered the shallow valley. She didn't start off running, though her pace grew faster. Her eyes locked on the slight curve ahead, the unseen dam, and claw-shaped fort at the end of her path.

Wind swept over her head, shifting the short locks of her hair. If she hadn't been jogging forward, her hair would have blocked her vision. Dust showered the air, especially when Lora left the driest patches of the valley. The shallow walls on both sides grew darker than she'd seen in too many gales.

Water loomed just out of reach. She smelled moisture in the air. It was close to the wet mist that rolled against the Ash Coasts. Such saturation was little more than a memory.

Above, the wind roared louder as another gale passed. Carson had likely drawn the attention of the Asurians in the fort. Even though another gale would come before Lora reached the outer bridge, fatigue still burdened her. No such limitation restrained her protector.

Turning her blade sideways, little Lora readied herself for Carson's attack.

He rolled under her sword and punched her in the gut. Air rushed away from her mouth. When Lora collapsed, Carson crouched beside her. "Don't clash your weapon. It's not a shield."

"I had to stop you to get an attack in."

"You're not going to stop me." Carson held his hand out for her. When Lora finally took it, he yanked her to her feet. "Use your enemy's movements against them. Everyone has a gap in their defense. Find that gap and exploit it."

Lora took a languished breath split between defeat and strain. "What if I can't find their weakness?"

"Then don't let them find yours."

As Lora approached the curve in the valley, a man's shape ambled far above on the high bridge. Even with the sunlight blasting upon her, a crimson sash drifted over the man's shoulder. A spear with gnarled edges stood as his constant companion. Without knowing which way the man would move, Lora stayed low and motionless.

She was a terrible hunter, not knowing when to strike. Lora preferred traps, especially since spears were noticeable and the Burning Hand used her life as kindling.

But she could wait. It was how she and Carson cornered enemies and prey. One flushed a target to rush toward the other. If Lora had been left to approach by herself, she'd have already dehydrated. Twice.

Footsteps crunched along the path Lora planned to take. Lora turned her attention downward, tilting her sword tips to the left before moving toward her destination. Two more Asurians walked from the fort toward the columns of fire.

Open flames made Lora's fingers tingle. She wanted to grab the flames and force them through the fort. If she could ride on wings of fire, Lora might take her rampage to the heart of Asuria itself.

The highest point on the right flaming column shook erratically.

Lora turned away, focusing on the path rising out of the shallow valley.

More seasons passed before Lora asked the question reviled by most travelers. "Are we there yet?"

"Are you excited to see Mono?"

Constant wandering had numbed Lora's mind. The same hazy crest lifted the horizon. Heat stirred any path they walked. Her stomach was always a pit of dull aches. Only a few small drinks of water satisfied her cravings. She didn't squat much, but she was more tired than ever.

"I'm sorry," Carson said. "I forgot what it means to travel in such young company."

"When do we get there?"

"In time, but not fast enough for whatever drives you."

"I said I'd go with you, just like Father said." All the tears had dried out of her eyes, even if her body wanted to shower them once again.

Carson nodded, shaking the wide folds of his dense black hood. "Build a fire. I will drive an animal toward you." He drew the weighty metal sword from his back, the held still. "No. You are still young and untrained."

"What do you want me to do?" She was eager to help if it got her away from the constant trails. Too long under the sun made anyone go mad.

"Can you tie a knot?"

She nodded.

"Can you make a snare?"

"I don't know."

Carson took a length of thin rope from his gear pack. He twisted the rope while explaining what he wanted. "You tie a little knot around a large loop of rope. When something steps into the loop, you pull the long end, closing a bigger knot. Does that make sense?"

Lora nodded as she took the slender rope and twisted it just the way Carson had suggested.

Far above Lora, Carson marched across the tall bridge. His sword and pauldron glowed brightly as they reflected so much of the sun's fury. He clashed with the spearman, who shouted with every sweep of their gnarly spear.

Lora slowed herself long enough to see the ground-based Asurians look up before running away. Reinforcements for the spearman overhead.

It was a bigger version of Carson's trap. Lora's job remained the same. When the target was in place, she'd pull the snare.

Rounding the last bend in the shallow valley, a tall pile of insect-ridden bodies rose above each rocky slope. Sand mixed with bloody muscle to forge a thick paste. The drippy smell of abandoned neighbors and slaughtered friends cooked into a steamy, wretched odor.

Asurians typically ate their victims and fashioned the remains into tools. They didn't build corpse walls where flesh acted like glue.

Immense reptilian bones criss-crossed from one human mound to the other. Breeze rolled over the makeshift draconic body of the dam. A cool hint of moisture touched Lora's nose. A clean scent finer than mist cut through the decay, offering a reminder that there was more to life and survival and death.

No child was meant to wait while holding a rope. Too many curiosities sent them off to explore, to create, to wander and get lost. Somehow, Lora made herself wait.

Her aching gut made her want to lie down, but the strain kept her from approaching sleep.

The wind blasted at her like the world kept breathing hot air. Tall, wispy weeds bent and bobbed whenever a gale blasted all around her. If Lora bent against as ifthe harsh breeze, she might topple over, never to rise again.

So she sat. Her eyes fixed on the wide loop she left untied. Sand danced over the woven fibers, a colorful blend of browns, blacks, and yellows. No rope had red fibers.

A buck-toothed critter with short dark gray fur waddled out of the thickest band of grass. The critter shifted back and forth on flattened, shovel-shaped hands topped with stubby bone claws. It had no tail. Only the weakest excuse for eyes framed the spike-shaped snout.

More out of confusion than instinct, Lora pulled her rope. It zipped shut around the critter's thick back legs. When it couldn't move, the strange animal bleated out a placid moan.

"Wonderful." Carson pushed his way through the grass. He dropped to his knees, stabbing the critter with a small ceramic knife.

Then it was quiet with the rest of the world.

Silence froze Lora's steps. Quiet threads of fire snaked around the charred blade in her right hand.

If the slightest flame congealed into a tight mass, Lora could destroy the dam in a single strike. She crouched and shuffled close to the base of the tower supporting the claw-shaped keep.

The steamy grasp reaching into the sky didn't seem right. Anything might hide inside. Whoever lurked within wanted something they couldn't simply reach out to take.

Weapons and armor collided. Shouts cut short. Crackling gurgles coughed through the air.

At the tip of Lora's charred blade, tongues of fire twisted in irritated braids. An ever-flowing ball of heat and annihilation warmed her knuckles and wrist.

Hesitation only stalled her and Carson. He made a distraction so Lora could do exactly what she'd prepared.

Angry shouts turned into a pair of battle cries on the high bridge.

Lora braced herself against the rocky terrain with her left forearm. She swung her right arm, letting the tangled knot of her fire launch toward the repurposed dragon's grave and the piles of human debris.

A stale body crashed beside her. A mass of armor and combat shaped too much like Carson.

Carson dug out a pit, filling it with a ring of small rocks around a twisted mound of grass. He told Lora to cut a line down the critter's belly, from its neck to its waist. The ceramic knife was sharp enough to slice through fur like it was cooled cheese. She made another cut across the animal's shoulders.

By then, Carson took over the cutting. Soon after, he'd stripped the skin and fur off the critter, wrapping what remained in a broad leaf. Once he pressed the critter against the mound of grass, Carson turned a smile full of ancient teeth toward Lora. "Ignite the bundle of grass."

"I don't have a flint."

"You are the flint. Open your right palm. Push your arm toward this pile of grass. If you offer a little of your life's fire, you can sustain yourself. Cooked food is better than raw meat."

The Burning Hand was death. It killed those it struck just as it would feed on Lora with every ember she spent.

"I can't."

"I won't make you, but the gift your parents have given you is the best way to ensure your survival."

"If I burn things, I'll die."

Carson tugged on his tapered beard. "Eventually, yes. I assure you, death is not something you can escape. You can only meet it on your terms."

Lora extended her hand. A surge of heat flooded her palm. The edges of her hand chilled, forcing her fingers to claw at the bundled critter and the mound of grass underneath.

Everything in the pit set on fire in the same instant. Stones acted as if they'd been soaked in oil. Severed vegetation crisped as every leaf danced with open flames.

The choking sound of laughter rumbled from the shadows around Carson's head. He tossed fresh rocks over the blazing pit. Cracked laughter surrounded his next command. "Scoop dirt over the fire. Fast as you can."

Sudden cold still clung to Lora's hand. If Carson hadn't shouted for her, she might have stayed in the same dull torpor. Her fingers batted erratic handfuls of dirt over the unburned rocks. Unearthed soil pushed cold against her fingertips, burrowing into her nails.

With the fire smothered, Carson sat back. His laughter softened as he collapsed on his side of the strange burial. "Now, wait two gales and we dig him back up."

"Why?"

"He's smoking right now. You'll see." Carson flopped onto his stomach. "For now, I rest."

Lora didn't fixate on Carson's collapsed mass. The Asurians she'd seen came running toward the crash site. Their fury fixed on her in a heartbeat.

Her confined rage exploded back toward them even faster. A single knight couldn't fight seasons of wandering. Lora needed a target to wound. She needed to hurt someone bearing the banners of the hated zealots. If they worshiped death, they deserved to die first.

Spears should have given them a greater reach. Lora lashed her Burning to the edge of her right blade, flinging it in a wide arc of ignition. Only the most dedicated fighter might hold their course when they'd spontaneously combusted. If the flames didn't feed on her own lifespan, she'd use them more often.

It was enough to hear the spearmen scream. They thrashed off balance. Each of them slapped at their tattered robes and woven bands of bone armor.

Lora pushed the tip of her left blade through one spearman's neck. She slashed another under the chin, letting them both tumble and gurgle.

If pouring them over Carson would bring him back, she'd have already done it. Her seasons-long companion was dead. No power in her understanding could change that. Not Xeryt, not even the banished heart of Tyrex.

Her world was death and chaos. The only counter to suffering was more suffering.

She marched toward the mangled dam of draconic debris. Human remains saturated the air, hardening Lora's decision.

She sheathed the burned blade. Her fingers flexed inward, drawing ambient heat out of the air. Fire spun, twisting into a thick knot of blazing hatred. The stench of baking rot blistered away from Lora's nose. Bits of ambient dust popped like blisters of smoke.

The scream of a child's wrath hardened into abandoned adulthood roared from Lora's grasp.

Steam erupted from the gap in the center of her hand. Wind boiled as it passed through the opening. Lora snapped her hand shut the instant moisture condensed in her palm.

Her eyes never left the fiery tangle, not even as it burrowed into the gaps between dragon bones. None of the dragon remains would burn; that was their gift.

But dead flesh and packed dirt did not share such virtue. Molten tar spurted from every fresh opening. Rather than be submerged, Lora's fires stretched out, taking root in every part of the horrid dam.

Lora clenched her teeth as her closed Burning Hand lifted. A thousand minute flames raced up from the barrier holding back the First River. Pain slashed through her wrist, burrowing toward her elbow.

She roared the anger she had swallowed ever since she had left the Ash Coasts behind.

Unlike her home, when the ground around the dam turned black, destruction followed.

Lora howled as loud as her expanding mouth would let her. She pressed her right hand over her face, trying to push the unleashed expression back into the safety of its cave.

She failed to quiet the anguish that begged for freedom season after season.

Waves of heavy wind shifted all around the young girl twice. Carson didn't move the entire time. He made no noise. His body refused to shift with a single breath.

Lora avoided touching him. Instead, she unearthed the smoldering collection of rocks and crisped grasses. Smoke rolled from the biggest rocks, especially the ring under the wrapped critter.

Carson's knife lay close to the bulk of his gear. Lora reached over the edge of the shallow pit, forgetting that any fire had been born of her own hand. The skin along the base of her palm flaked with desiccation. Grooves in the center of her hand webbed with lines as dark as the most scorched ashes she'd ever seen.

As her stomach rumbled, Lora snatched up the knife and cut the leaf wrapped around the critter. Savory steam flushed away from the small body. She cut a chunk off the critter's back leg. Unable to hesitate, she gobbled up the bit of cooked flesh before sitting up in shock.

The critter was delicious.

Lora's hunger set her to cutting off bit after bit, leaving next to nothing of the critter behind when she was done.

Only then did the knight shamble into a seated position. He pushed back on the weight of his hood, exposing bands of muscle and tendon stretched beyond anything natural. Much of his face still had sections of skin, especially his bearded jawline. Carson's eyes were lidless, almost like hungry birds had pecked away the tissue.

Attention filled his gaze. He snapped his hood forward. "I'm sorry for that. I should have warned you."

Lora glared at the blackened web expanding from the hole in her right hand. "I should have saved you more to eat."

"That's not necessary, Lora." He shifted around the pit, collecting his ceramic knife. "I don't need to eat or drink. The scholars of Shabra-Lai animated me ages ago. I'll keep going as long as they want me to go."

"What does that mean?"

"I'm already dead, Lora. I have been for a long time."

Bodies bobbed up and down as the river opened wide. The air cooled. Soft moisture filled the released breeze.

The First River raced with an uncanny freshness. If it had been any other aquatic passage, Lora would have hesitated to plunge her head beneath the rolling waves. The crisp, saltless sensation refreshed her face and relaxed her eyes. She swallowed several gulps before rising in a welcome fit of coughing.

Lora nearly set herself to drinking, but another weighty corpse swayed up and down with the reborn tide. She lunged into the water, grasping at the hooded collar around Carson's neck. The blistered, partially rotten face rolled back and forth.

If he fell beneath the waves, they might be no getting him back. Metal acted like an oppressive rock, always sinking to the bottom of any waterway.

Lora's grip pulled the tendons of her left hand far too tight. She couldn't risk letting go. She didn't understand what kept Carson going, but his loyalty was always to her. If not her, then to Father. Or to whatever mysticism that fueled him.

Soreness flooded her shoulder blades faster than the First River reclaimed the shallow valley it already dug through the world. An empty groan rumbled in her throat as she flopped against the rocky bank, tossing her lifeless companion onto a dry surface.

No restorative breath would resurrect Carson. He didn't breathe, never ate, and refused to drink. His animation was a gift Lora couldn't decipher. All she knew was to cover his face.

Of all the beings in the world, Carson reviled the sun most of all.

Lora sat by the rolling water, taking some time to refresh her stores. She kept a trail cup in her bag, a ruby chunk of glass that echoed the ambient light of the chamber where her family had last been together. Lora scooped water from the river, drinking out of desperation and abundance. Any parasite would find her a poor meal.

The claw-shaped tower stood with the same authority it held before. Steam and light burst from the elongated fingertips, stretching as if they meant to claw through the sky itself.

"It's not done," Lora said, her eyes focused upon the sky.

"Go." Carson's voice cracked through the hood Lora had draped over his face. Anything resembling life within the knight urged Lora onward.

Whatever caused the death at Lai Cross still reached out from the tower.

For the fourth time in a single season, young Lora passed close to the burned husk of a caravan. Mantorse husks crumbled like ashen eggshells. Wagons lay half melted in crumbled ruins. Most of the death stink had already fluttered away with some earlier gale.

At the head of the fallen caravan, several crimson-robed corpses with black sashes lay abandoned to the elements.

Lora flexed her right hand, wishing it wasn't wasteful to burn them with her own fire. Instead, she kicked a skinny corpse. The body wheezed like an old man's fart. She clamped a hand over her face and snapped away.

After a long groan, Lora found Carson approaching. "Just because a corpse is thin doesn't mean it's not bloated."

"Found that out the hard way."

"Then I hope you learned the lesson."

Lora shook her head. "Someone should have already killed the Asurians."

Carson turned one corpse's face back and forth before checking another. "Do you know this symbol?" He pointed at a black sunburst burned onto a slain face. The same emblem marred the other Asurian corpses.

For half a breath, Lora thought it was the mark of Xeryt. The gap in her right hand was more diamond-shaped than it was a sunburst. Carson found seemed to be an inverted version.

"Whoever did that did the world a favor."

"Maybe." Carson let the bodies go. "It seemed odd to me."

"When we see them, we can thank them." Lora's right hand itched for a moment before she left the slain Asurians behind as well.

Walking back to the clawed tower took at least an entire gale. The wind spat around Lora, but she kept moving, refreshed by the restored water.

A serrated spear was lodged in a jagged bank of sharp stones. Chunks of loosened dragon bone drifted along the river. Those who crafted death and misery lingered only as broken debris.

Water dripped from an arched opening in the tower's base. A barbed sheet of ripped leather flapped against the saturated passage. Light refused to enter, rejected by a constant gurgling hiss.

Any measure of life spent breathing radiated the burned blade. Dim radiance made no difference under the great bridge's shadow. After walking up a few of the spiraling stone stairs, the ambient flame along the narrow cutting edge turned Lora into a beacon in the dark.

She never considered such things. With the people in Lai Cross already dead, they'd never present her with gratitude. Her family was far behind her on the trail of maturity. She never expected to find any sacred cities. Not Carson's home in the sky, not some rumored land of acceptance defended by a throat-slasher, and certainly not some place only accessible through a dragon's guidance.

The only hope Lora inspired was living for another gale, maybe as long as a season.

Onyx stones supported her feet as she rose through the winding passage. With such shadows, no sun worshipper would venture enter on a whim. Zealots preferred their beliefs, else they'd run in cowardice.

After Lora's knees and thighs had screamed loud enough, the twisting darkness stopped rising. Another arch led her into a widened chamber with food stores aligned on her left, gurgling pipes chugging to her right. Between them, two doors hung open and forgotten, exposing the tower to anything the high bridge might have offered.

Lora shook her head at the vacated sight before taking a slender stairway close to the noisy pipes.

The angry tubes split apart, rising in six new directions.All of them twisted toward a widened chamber with a makeshift sunlight knocked in the top of it. Five elevated tunnels curled upward, leading to the artificial fingers clawing toward the sky. Two pools framed a sunburst-shaped platform that echoed the moment Lora's happiness had been murdered.

"Why?" A crone's voice rose from the far side of the chamber. "I had nearly carved part of the world away from the Asurian war machine. I crafted enough death for me to attract some of their loyalists."

"You choked a town."

The crone stood. Her dress bore the faded reds and blacks. A sooty burst emblem rested upon her brow. "What's one town against the tide of savagery and murder?"

"You can't even hear yourself." Lora shook her head as she moved closer to the crone. "I've seen your mark before."

"We sacrificed many who served the false sun." Sharpened fingernails pointed at Lora. "You aren't even Asurian. Why care?"

The question hovered over Lora. She'd asked herself the same thing every season, wondering why she hadn't settled in a town she'd passed. Some had peace, but she avoided it. Nor for loyalty or to remember her family. "Asurians killed my family. Killed my home. I have no peace."

The crone elevated her hand toward the open passages above them. "With enough water, this artifice would pluck the light from the sun. Another piece would fall, creating another realm of night."

Lora approached, wary of any traps. There was only the sunburst upon a central altar, a vulgar aquatic version of the Temple of the Burning Hand.

One of the crone's sharpened fingers snapped at Lora. "You must know it well. Part of the sun fell. The seaside where the shard fell became the Ash Coasts."

Lora lifted her blades to attack. Edged flames lit the crone's cloudy gray-blue eyes.

"I know the Burning Hand. They must have pierced you as a child."

Lora didn't answer.

"There was a time when I faked Asurian devotion. I sent death to the Ash Coasts." The glimmer of a sunburst-shaped crystal lay embedded within the crone's hand. "Tyrex commanded it."

The dark faith whispered between the children of Pyre. False disciples who perverted the flames.

Lora ran her burned blade through the crone. Embers of flame sparked from the old woman's tear ducts. The crone grinned and laughed, so Lora slashed with the pristine blade.

Blood showered from the spontaneous fountain, smothering the trails of fire pumping through the archaic body.

∞

Five seasons before the Asurians came to the Ash Coasts, little Lora stumbled to knit a single stitch. A woven green back hanging on the opposite side of the Temple of the Burning Hand inspired her the most. It was one of the few places where Lora could keep to herself.

Only Father bothered looking for her in such a sacred place. "You're always determined to be in here."

"It's quiet and cuddly. It's a good place to knit."

Father came closer. "What are you knitting?"

"I'm just trying to copy this bag." Lora pointed to an old sack hanging beyond the sour and steamy lava barrier.

He picked Lora up. His voice turned timid. "Let's not worry about that bag."

"Why?"

"It's old and mean. Left over from a different version of the world."

"Oh." Lora didn't understand, but she didn't want to upset Father.

"Let's find you something else to knit instead."

Lora's eyes lit up. She'd find some help. "I like that."

❧

Eventually, Lora shifted down the spiral stairs and ventured back into the sun. Carson sat hunched over, keeping the light away from his face.

She pushed through the last acidic hint of dehydration on her tongue. "Did you know what I'd find?"

Carson stood, restraining when an answer would come. "I'd felt the sensation in the tower before. When I saw the old woman's hand, I understood."

Lora's scowl hung heavy, even with the deed finished. "Crazy bitch thought she could tear the sun apart."

"Or she wanted to steal the water for herself."

"I don't care which." Lora lifted the bag she'd made by cutting the crone's robes. Lora had severed the woman's hand instead of touching the crystal. "Mind carrying this for me?"

"This once." Carson took the bag, making sure the rival powers didn't occupy too close a space.

GENESIS SONG

In the world's birth cry
Earth and sky were one and same
The sun burned delight
A line was drawn no further
Fire, heat singed the horizon

Around the sun forged
A space where saddened wind blew
Soil divided
Baking desolate lonely
A bright sun burned far apart

No matter the wind
No matter the rain or snow
Relief never came
Overhead light burned always
Searing sadness forever

A break in the pain
Light dimmed in one realm of view
A spot of true dark
Not a place hidden in ground
Not a field wet with rain clouds

A howl of thunder
The sky all clear or obscured
The hatchling of life
Wings proud upon the expanse
Wyrms of a rainbow fly free

Fracture turmoil
Come, embrace the litany
Newborn beast of sky
Humans clinging to the ground
Gods of the lowest dungeon

Speak at the apex
Let your faith endure always
Sing of life given
Make true the promise of old
Earth, sky, and sun united.

Fanatics
Rise up
Evil burns the blood
Enmity burns the soul
Doom comes from despair
Order serves the worst barbarians
Madness is surrender.

Some wounds
Heal in ways to set us
Apart from others
Bound to offer hope,
Radiance, and compassion.
All are worthy.
Love how you will
Admire what is
Inspire a better world.

A CONVERSATION IN FOUR PARTS

Thirty-two Seasons Prior to the Ascension

Pillars of smoke rose from the mountains protecting the Ash Coasts. Crimson and black banners stood high. Emblems of the Charred Hand burned away every local hope and dream.

Vanity gripped the protective railing high above the Charred Temple. As an Illumina, she dressed in soot-washed white silks, shook her head. Her hair never deviated from the perfect wave rolling over her shoulders.

Vanity's lips did not pout seductively. Her frown hovered over the city of the pyromancers, but the Asurian army did not notice.

Beside her, a playful voice drew close. "Sister, you seem bothered."

Vanity opened her mouth to answer but looked down instead. Men tore apart merchant carts with the same ferocity they attacked fertile pyromancers.

"I hear screaming and tears. There is only anguish."

The other Illumina, Purity, stood against Vanity. Her hands pressed the same flame-crusted railing. "Soon they will convert or find mercy in the Death He Brings."

"I've been here for gales. Their torment only grows."

"Once the battle ends—"

"Have you seen a single flame reach one of our dragons?"

"Not since the battle started. Our army fell on the pyromancers. Helio-Asura washes us with glory."

Vanity leaned toward the carnage around the temple. "Purity, that's not glory down there. It's conquest, rape, and plunder. Every Imperia and Imperion will overflow, but who will be left to convert?" Vanity raised her hands in offering to the sun, even though smoke and clouds blocked the sky. "What pyromancer will praise our God after this?"

The sly smile fell from Purity's face. She kissed Vanity's onyx gauge and whispered. "Atsuko."

Vanity pulled away, shaking her head. "No. No. I gave her up. I am Vanity—"

Purity pressed her fingertips over Vanity's lips. "There is only carnage and death around us. I am not meant for this."

Relaxing her arms and jaw, Vanity waited for Purity to release her. "You… sound like a non-believer."

"I'm not meant for this."

"What does that mean, Purity? Can you still call yourself that?"

"The Illumina had dug her talons deep into both of us. When she remade you, she filled me with hope. Seeing this…" Purity gestured at the city bristling with chaos. "Her spell over me is broken."

Vanity pressed a hand over her companion's shoulder. "Maybe something can be done. We can bring people mercy."

Purity pressed a mark embedded under her ear. "I can't touch anyone's mind, much less give them mercy."

"You don't need some power to spread mercy and hope."

"We're Illumina. Our purpose is to blind people to everything that doesn't serve Sorcha Kagatsu."

"Don't say her name like that."

"What? You're not convinced of your mission, but you'll still support the woman who led you astray?" Purity shook her head. "We all wear soiled robes now. She can hide it, but we can't. As long as we are Illumina, we'll wear white." Purity pulled the soot-crusted veil away from her face. "Do you want to serve a tyrant blindly? Or would you prefer a calling away from her voice?"

Quiet in her own cocoon, Vanity pushed her conviction aside. Purity may have called her by a dead name, but the sound still took Vanity's breath away.

Purity lowered her veil and went inside, out of the sun.

Sixty-one Seasons Prior to The Ascension

High above the world, heat became a frigid concept. Atsuko knew about the zones, but never considered what it would be like to stand in one for a moment or even a full gale. Under Mountain Kagatsu, a fresh season of Monsoon rolled past, denying water to anyone looking down from the clouds.

As she watched the world, Atsuko's shoulders sank under the sweltering sun. If she could, Atsuko would have shaved her head, denying the sweat another place to latch onto her. Perspiration gripped both halves of her face, caring nothing for her deformity.

A simple top and a tiny skirt were the only clothing the Imperia allowed any of the women to wear. Exposure let the sun hammer more of Atsuko's skin into hardened bronze.

The other initiates stood along the edge of the mountain, all swaying with exhaustion.

"Only four more of you must fall," Purity said, her voice echoing behind them. "Think of what you will be. Radiant. Powerful. Luminous. To shine so bright, you must endure."

A girl barely old enough to menstruate wheezed and slipped. Her knee hovered over the rocky surface, refusing to bow to the elements.

From the behind Atsuko, a woman her own age called out. "Give up already. You can jump if you don't want to go to the larder."

If there was any moisture left in Atsuko's body, her mouth would have watered. Her stomach had been barren for so long, the idea of food filled her with agony and joy.

Atsuko's fingers curled into fists. Her eyes bore into Purity's side. Still, Atsuko did not strike. Atsuko did not speak. The aching purr of her stomach would not bear it.

"Let go," Purity said with compassion. "Only the most hardened need to bear this world. Accept Helio-Asura's mercy and reward."

"It won't work." Atsuko's eyes shot up. She hadn't thought, only spoke.

Purity stepped away from the girl, grinning as she approached Atsuko. Before she spoke, Purity took a half-step back. "Did you dip your face in lava as a child?"

Atsuko's mouth curled downward. "Born this way."

"How does a freak know what can work? You've got an eye where your cheek should be."

"I've fought to live just like anyone else." Atsuko tensed, leaning toward Purity. "Do you want her to live or die?"

"This challenge is supposed—"

"Do you want her to live or die?" Atsuko pushed the words out, forcing her voice to enunciate more with each syllable.

Purity eyed Atsuko, looking up and down. No one could decide what eye to focus on. "I'll make sure someone falls. As long as that happens, the Imperia is happy."

"Are you happy?" Atsuko asked. She glanced over Purity's shoulder as the girl's ankle slipped again.

Chuckling, the woman shook her head. "Happiness is something that children have to blind themselves from reality."

A heavy bead of sweat ran down the bridge of Atsuko's nose. "Give me your knife."

"Giving up?"

"Just do it."

Purity pulled the blade from her belt. She slowly pushed the handle toward Atsuko. "I'm curious."

Atsuko touched the blade, pulling the thin air into her lungs. Her gaze met the stern angle of Purity's eyes. Releasing a short breath, Atsuko coiled her fingers around the handle. She turned her wrist, treating the sharpened bone as an extension of herself.

Prowling toward the weary girl, Atsuko looked at the mountain for an instant. A feminine shape draped in crimson and black stared back, robbing Atsuko's ability to breathe. Locking her jaw tight, she continued her approach.

Purity looked on, playing with a curl of her upswept hair.

Atsuko tensed her fingers until her knuckles stung from holding the small blade. Her left hand opened wide as she raised her arm. She clutched the girl's hair, jerking hard enough to pull several strands from the scalp. The girl glanced back, unable to blink. Atsuko hesitated, noting the girl's symmetrical, heart-shaped face.

Closing her eyes, Atsuko stabbed the girl's neck. Drawing the blade from left to right, Atsuko heard the same wet gurgle that came from the old and infirm. A sticky spray drenched Atsuko's hands. When the moisture stopped flowing, she breathed in once more.

"Initiative." Purity nodded, holding out a hand. "The Imperia likes that."

Atsuko passed the blade back without looking at the bloodied girl.

Around the edge, Asurian guards taunted the other initiates.

Purity sheathed the blade and waved for Atsuko to follow her. "Come on—and bring the girl. We have lots of work to do."

In the Eightieth Season of Heika Kori,
Goddess of the Elements

Dressing in dragon weave did nothing to protect Atsuko from the cold. A chill dug into the thin calluses on her feet. She'd forgotten what it was like to walk on the ground rather than soar through the sky.

Frost latched onto Atsuko's breath. Ice crusted over the distant walls and framed the long bridge leading to the Ivory Throne.

The shape of a woman hovered over the Ivory Throne, nestled within a web of icicles woven around crystallized pyres. The creature on the throne quietly regarded Atsuko with glistening eyes of scorched black. Snow pale skin sculpted the woman's delicate cheeks while onyx lips flexed—the first sign of life she offered.

Fear crept into every pause before the locals spoke the name of Heika Kori. They said she kept a wall of winter overhead to block the oppressive sunlight. They said she willed ice to form during monsoons and fire to ignite in freezing weather.

Atsuko lowered her head in a slight bow. "Heika Kori, Goddess of the Seasons, I have come—"

"Asurian." Heika Kori's voice snapped like the surface of a frozen lake. "Your kind has never been welcome here."

Atsuko straightened herself. "I am not the same as the others."

"The same red hair. The same bronzed skin. I have seen it before. I have seen it on Sorcha Kagatsu's altar, just as I see it on your perfect face. Did you steal that face yourself or did you beg your mistress to make you whole?"

"Whole?" Atsuko turned her head away. They called Heika Kori a Goddess, but it couldn't actually be possible.

"Did you beg her when you were on her mountain or later when she took you to her city?"

Atsuko stepped back, easing her hand toward the sheathed blade on her hip. "I have come on behalf of the Alliance of Nations—"

A column of ice burst up from the Ivory Throne, lifting Heika Kori. "Answer me, Vanity. How much of your soul did you sell to Sorcha Kagatsu?"

"I didn't sell my soul."

"Then you gave it freely. I saw you trade it for silks and a white veil. I watched you revel in a shower of blood as you accepted a murderess into your heart."

"I did no… such…" Atsuko lowered her hands, stepped closer once again. "Goddess, would you… grin for me?"

Heika Kori's brow tilted downward. "What?"

"Grin. Smirk. A playful smile of some kind."

A tiny giggle popped out of the Goddess's mouth.

Atsuko shook her head. "You convinced me that you were—"

"A goddess?" Heika Kori smirked for an instant. The chill stripped her face of warmth, leaving her glossy stare intact.

"How? How did you do it, Purity?"

Heika Kori slipped back onto her throne. "You did not answer me, Asurian. How much of your soul belongs to Sorcha Kagatsu?"

"You know I doubted her."

"But I was the one who left." The Goddess extended her arms, allowing ice to clothe her in more layers of white and blue. "Answer me, Asurian, or I will give you nothing."

Atsuko closed her eyes, watching the Ash Coasts burn with fire rather than smolder in embers. The trampled screamed in her ears, begging to be saved. Instead of reaching down to them, she'd watched as more dragons rushed through the city. She witnessed imperia and imperion walk through the streets, drinking in death.

"I gave her enough to go to another city and rule it in her name." Atsuko turned away, clutching the golden fibers wrapped around her body.

"You relished death like an imperia. You ordered the last of the Dancers killed—"

Closing her fists and locking her teeth together, Atsuko snapped forward. "I killed the last Dancer myself. Easier than I killed the girl on the mountain." Air raced in and out of Atsuko's nose. "Easier than watching the Imperia toy with that man on the Altar. You know the one."

Heika Kori's breath chilled the air as it left her nose and mouth. She nodded. "I remember."

"Then you remember it was you who supported me, made me content to wear that veil and those silks." Atsuko pointed up and down her body. "I'm not wearing them now and nor are you."

Crystallized fire flickered through the chamber, never giving way to the freezing shadows. Atsuko watched her opposite. Sister, Goddess, loyal Illumina.

Opening her hands, Atsuko stood next to the ice skirted around Heika Kori. "These hands have done everything you have done. When you ask how much of my soul belongs to the Imperia, do you ask yourself as well?"

"I know where I stand."

Atsuko offered her hands. "We may have taken different paths, but we are still very much the same."

Curled fingers rose from the Ivory Throne. "I am fire and wind and ice."

"I was born for my dragon. He was born for me." Atsuko gave her fallen friend a small smile. "Those are the paths we have taken. They aren't who we are."

"Perhaps." Heika Kori pressed her hands against Atsuko's.

The frosty chill bit Atsuko's fingers, but she held on all the same. "Perhaps."

Fifty-eight Seasons Prior to the Ascension

Sinewy towers rose throughout the Holy City of Helion. At the heart of the city, the highest tower of all grasped desperately at Helio-Asura Himself. The gleaming sun washed over Vanity's symmetrical heart-shaped face—the ideal gift for a woman who had proven her devotion.

As the horns sounded, Vanity took a deep breath, steeling herself before taking the first steps up the narrow stairs that led to the Blooded Altar. Vanity had sacrificed before, but never at the holiest point of her faith.

A short line of bodies in frayed scraps of leather followed the path. Vanity gripped the handle of her bone knife, pressing its warm danger against her skin. The others ahead of her had done similar, but none of them held their tools as tight or stood in awe. Each of them was ugly and misshapen. Some hobbled on clubbed feet. None of them had been sculpted by the Imperia's perfect hand. They couldn't possibly know the glory of Helio-Asura.

Grinning, Vanity felt her purpose. A trail of blood crept between the crafted globes on Vanity's chest. Opening her full lips, she whispered her prayer. "Praise Helio-Asura. Praise His heat and light. Praise the Death He Brings." The wound closed, though no one ahead of Vanity exalted the power of their god.

"I accept my purpose," Vanity said at full volume. "It is death."

Her knife lunged forward, piercing the supplicant's side. Vanity shoved the wounded beast onto the steps and scrambled onward. The wet blade slashed through skin and tendon, allowing Vanity to push the wounded off the high tower. She hoped the scraps of strength rose from the hideous creatures and empowered the Imperia.

But it was not the highest of priestesses who waited for Vanity at the top.

The curled, satisfied grin of Purity rarely faded, even for an instant. Clad in layers of pristine white silk, Purity clasped her hands together. "My calling is the Death He Brings."

Vanity lay her drenched knife at Purity's feet, then pressed her forehead on the highest step. "I have come to answer the call."

"Would you be infused with light?"

"Light or death, I would do anything for my god." Vanity's heart raced. The Imperia's lessons clutched her heart, purified her soul. Vanity no longer wore the asymmetric face of disbelief. She understood rightness, correctness.

Looking up, the elegant demeanor Purity proudly wore filled Vanity with joy.

From behind the cloaked peak of the Altar, another woman spoke. "One dressed in filth cannot be infused with light."

Purity grabbed the Vanity's worn top, ripping it like an old rag. In her exposure, Vanity forgot to breathe. She released a slight sigh when Purity pulled away the lower scrap of leather too. As Purity tossed away the torn strips, she pushed Vanity against the stained slab, the Blooded Altar itself.

Imperia Sorcha Kagatsu stepped around the peak of the Altar. Sharp black talons extended from the priestess's fingers. Her scarlet mane danced up into the prongs of an extensive onyx crown before falling to her waist. Rather than wear robes of dragon weave, the Imperia outlined her curves in a thin wrap of deep maroon.

"Vanity." Each syllable glided from the Imperia's mouth with floral sweetness. "You are as I have sculpted you, but I can only shape you. Tell me what is in your heart."

Collapsing to her knees, Vanity opened her arms. "My heart is dark and empty."

"Then let us fill it."

The Imperia pulled the cloak away from the peak, exposing the grand Mirror of Tila. Already at a slight angle, the sun washed over Vanity from two points. Illuminated, she cried out.

In the light, Vanity waited, beaming under the direct attention of the Imperia, of Asuria as a whole.

"We must seal the light inside you." The Imperia pulled on a chain, dragging a muscular man from behind the Mirror. Kagatsu tightened the man's bonds, shackling him on top of the Altar. The man flailed impotently, helping Purity rip away another set of clothing.

The Imperia eclipsed the sun and the man alike. Her body shifted and contorted, wordlessly calling upon Helio-Asura vitality and power. As the Imperia's voice stretched into the sky, her talons fell upon the man's neck.

Limp, the man's life drained over Vanity and into the Imperia.

When the shower finished, the Imperia rose from the Altar. Light swelled into Vanity's eyes again, bristling her skin with ecstasy.

Purity wiped the splatter from Vanity's face and skin, leaving her hair wet with blood.

The Imperia pressed a talon under Vanity's chin, easing her upward. "You have been washed anew."

"I am cleansed with light and blood." Vanity did not blink, staring intently at the Imperia's constant gaze.

"The Light of Helio-Asura is bonded to you now. This Light elevates you."

Vanity lifted her arms toward the sun. "Praise Helio-Asura."

"You are now Illumina."

Purity swept around Vanity, wrapping her flesh in layers of unblemished white silk. The Imperia pressed a golden tiara into Vanity's billowing hair just as a drop of blood smeared her brow.

Vanity stood, smiling as Purity smiled, feeling identical, as one. Simultaneously, both Illuminae swept their veils forward and knelt before their mistress.

"You will be nourished," the Illumina said, "then you will take your light into other nations."

A PRAYER FROM BENEATH

Free me now
Demon old
Liberate
Heat and Sound

Boil that dream
Innocence
Fool skies
and the folly of light.

Climb, I would not
Gifts be damned
My soul binds
Far above.

Hers is hated
Newest realm of all
My patience
Ran at last.
Askew.

MIGHTY WINGS

Arcs of lightning raced through the tunnel of ever-darkening gray clouds. Thunder was constant. Waves of rain flooded the sky.

Even so, Norrin raced on, clinging tighter to Shara's back. The blue dragon's wings batted as hard as the thunder just to keep from falling to the long lost ground.

Another roar trembled behind them. With the spinning storm, Norrin couldn't risk glancing over his shoulder.

Water sprayed at his eyes. Shara growled.

Norrin patted the leathery flesh around Shara's node. In his thoughts, Norrin said, "I hear you, friend. You know the way home."

A shadow drifted over spiraling cloud bank. Two pairs of narrow wings clasped together in a single sail. "Laktus. He's the only one bold enough to fly through here."

Shara gave an amused grunt.

"Besides us, yes. Keep the to lowest part of the cloud tunnel."

The shadow turned, drifting for an instant before separating the wings on one side. The narrow-winged dragon turned to intercept Norrin and Shara.

Shara growled and grunted.

Norrin hugged Shara's back, pushing the node on his wrist against the matching mass on the blue dragon's back. The young man touched the loaded pouch strapped to his leg, reminding himself of the prize inside.

Laktus sat upright on his mount, the aged Sag-An. For a hundred seasons, they waited at the border of Ortica, driving off any who were unwelcome in the kingdom. Laktus wore a barbed helmet carved from a fallen black dragon. Sag-An wore extra plates of armor, all stolen from his slain foes.

Lifting a bladed pike, Laktus crouched as Norrin had a moment earlier.

"We have to get to the Prince," Norrin said, convincing himself of his purpose. "Go."

Shara roared as did Sag-An. The aged dragon raced forward. Shara flapped both pairs of wings, bursting downward. A streak of lightning ruptured around both beasts, causing them to cry out.

"Push into the edge."

Grumbling, Shara drifted into the twisting bank of gray clouds.

Sheets of rain slapped Norrin's face, but it couldn't be helped. To stay in the heart of the tunnel would invite an even more severe attack.

Sag-An rushed over Norrin, snapping meaty talons as the aged dragon passed. Norrin didn't rise, dodging the tip of Laktus's pike as it jabbed downward.

Instinct pushed out of Shara, filling Norrin with the impulse to attack. For an instant, they gave in.

Shara's wings locked together, opening into a wide sail. The blue dragon swept upward, smashing into Sag-An's rear wings.

The aged dragon's tail scraped along Norrin's side in the collision. No blood was drawn, but Norrin knew there would be a wide bruise for some time.

Below Shara, Sag-An spun, flapping his wings, bleating like a sheep. Laktus dangled with one arm on his mount, the other still holding the pike.

Norrin took a long exhale and tightened his grip. The impulse to pursue swelled in his thoughts, but he clenched his teeth and pushed it away. "To Ortica, and the Prince."

Shara rose in the tunnel, soaring through the clearest path to the aerie.

Gales passed, each blasting away more of the saturation in Norrin's shirt. Near the pouch holding the prize, the cotton didn't feel damp, nor had it.

Clouds dispersed, unfolding the tunnel into a wide expanse. Shara was too far up for either of them to see the horizon ahead or above. Only the sun's heat, power, and majesty was allowed. The constant of all life, aside from fables.

Below, rippling over the wide cast of ocean, Norrin spotted a dot soaring at an angle from where Shara flew. Norrin didn't need to see much of the dragon to know it was the same painted beast as before. Sag-an had lived through wars, only serving the most determined of riders. No rider more determined than Laktus.

"Can you find an island?" Norrin asked.

Shara barked, almost like she was spitting.

Norrin opened one of his supply sacks, touching a pale white mass. His fingers slipped around the grip, pressing the toggle. The buzzer clicked once since it hadn't been primed.

Hooking her wings together, Shara climbed to a higher altitude.

Norrin closed the sack and held tight to the dragon's back. He glanced upward, cringing at the wind whipping his eyes and cheeks.

Nestled between rays of gleaming light and the palest blue sky, a lone island floated above. The tiny brown island bore only a single scraggly tree over a patch of bare ground. An outcropping of bedrock dangled underneath, keeping the mass from floating or falling into oblivion.

With a slight pull, Norrin steered Shara to the lowest part of the island. "Steady, Shara. Stay close." Norrin reached into the pack again, pulling out the buzzer and a strip of ceramic barbs. He slammed the strip into the base of the buzzer, then turned a crank on the side of the wide shaft. Gripping the weapon with both hands, Norrin breathed in and squeezed the toggle. In the time it took to exhale, the barbs flew out like a swarm of insects, each chewing into the narrow at the bottom of the island.

After slapping in another strip of barbs, Norrin stashed the buzzer again. "Down. Let's pick a fight."

Threads of white rushed against Norrin's face as Shara swept down. The dragon folded all four wings inward, exposing only a slight flap to stay on target.

Sag-an glided on a rising course. Undisturbed, Laktus would urge a corkscrew turn to stay in the air current leading to Ortica.

Norrin lay against Shara, hugging the dragon's armor. The edge of a large plate bit into Norrin's cheek. He kept his gaze ahead, using Shara's horn to aim.

Slapping Shara's side charged an inferno within the dragon. Shara's body shook. Norrin clutched the straps binding him to the dragon's back. He pulled harder, tensing his knuckles where he couldn't let go.

He needed no connection with Shara. When Sag-an became clear, Shara opened her mouth spewing bile upon the aged dragon. On contact, the liquid ignited. The impact shook Sag-an off course.

Shara's wings opened as she curled her body. The wind and momentum pushed the dragon upward. A fierce beating of wings shot her and Norrin toward the sun once again.

Norrin leaned back, watching the aged dragon tumble. Painted wings flapped frantically, but victory seemed implausible.

A section of armor fell away from the aged dragon, propelling Sag-an and Laktus into pursuit.

"Higher, Shara. They're coming."

Sag-an roared from below. Shara thundered her wings harder, never looking away from the island overhead.

Norrin coughed as they drew close, breathing in dust from the rock he'd blasted. As Shara swooped in an arc around the top of the island, Norrin asked, "Ready?"

Shara barked in approval, turning in an arc even closer to the island.

Norrin jumped. His boots landed on a platform of hardened dirt. Cracks clawed through the surface, having baked under the sun for countless seasons without rain. Gripping the buzzer, Norrin cranked the weapon knowing he would need to use it soon enough.

If he didn't, the barbs would shake loose, firing anywhere they could.

Twisting in a corkscrew, Sag-an flew over the island, letting his armored rider leap jump down. Laktus kept his spear pointed upward. With a bellowing voice, Laktus made the wind go silent. "Do you have the token?"

"I do." Norrin's gaze shifted toward the pouch on his leg for an instant.

"Good trick with the breath attack. I haven't been caught like that since the war." Laktus pulled off his helmet, setting it on the ground long enough to wipe sweat from the top of his shaved head. Deep lines weathered the warrior's face, from age, from exposure, a few from battle.

"Will you let me take the token to our Prince?"

"No boy is worthy of our Prince." Laktus shifted the helmet back over his head. "It doesn't matter if you've been to the Night Lands. Give me the shard and I'll remember your efforts."

Norrin pulled in a thin breath only. Dampness rushed through his scalp, sagging his brow. He knew how much the heat would smash into him, but had forgotten it during his time in the dark. Traveling to such a cool and comfortable place was a fabled notion. Norrin only left because the Prince—

Laktus lifted his spear once more and charged.

One side of the island lifted with a wide sharp-edged rock but remained flat otherwise. The confined flat plane gave Norrin nowhere to run just as it gave Laktus every path to charge.

As he shifted into a defensive stance, Norrin smiled at his charging enemy. "Shara!"

The blue dragon curled in a circle and swooped underneath the island. The ground shook and Laktus lost his footing for a moment.

Norrin raced away from Laktus, jumping from the island. The chunk he'd shot at fell down through the clouds. Shara rolled, fanning her wings to stay under Norrin.

Sag-an roared as he flapped after them. Each beat of the aged dragon's wings erupted like thunder.

Norrin's arms flailed. Two fingers slipped off the buzzer's grip. Wind smashed against his nose and lips. Eventually, his body would smash against the sea.

Above Norrin, the aged dragon roared again. A dim orange glow bubbled around the beast's mouth. Droplets strung dangled out from Sag-an's teeth.

Shara's tail zipped back and forth, drifting away from Norrin's grasp. Norrin reached for his buzzer anyway.

The ocean widened, expanding along more of the visible horizon. All the landmasses overhead vanished in the sun's glare.

With a grunt, Norrin, pulled his left hand toward the buzzer, shoving the weapon in place again. He turned, lining the tip of the buzzer with Sag-an's side.

Squeezing the grip, barbs jumped from the buzzer. Each pointed dart dug into Sag-an's right wings, burrowing into the gaps of the dragon's armor. Sag-an howled, releasing a mouth half full of liquid fire.

Norrin abandoned the buzzer, twisting to find Shara before Sag-an's breath could find them.

Shara roared to Norrin's left. Burning droplets landed on the blue dragon's skin.

Norrin folded his arms against his sides, bulleting himself at the dragon. Open air continued to thrash at him while the ocean reached toward them from below.

Sag-an's wings flared out, stopping the aged dragon's descent. Flaming globs still hurled around Norrin and Shara. One flaming thread tore into Norrin's leg. The pain jerked his arm back from Shara's side.

He had to make sure the Prince's prize had not fallen away.

The blue dragon barked. Even with more droplets burning Shara, she was the only way to evade the ocean.

Norrin clawed at Shara's armor, snagging one of the saddle straps. "Climb!"

Holding on for all life, Norrin's perspective twisted. Shara spun to evade the rest of Sag-an's scattered attack. Norrin's eyes said up was to his side, his stomach said up was below him. Norrin shut his eyes, burped, and pulled himself toward Shara.

The dragon knew the way, but Norrin said it to relieve himself. "Ortica."

Once the inertia finished with Norrin, he glanced upward, watching the distant island drift toward the sun. A flailing dot kept rushing toward the mass, refusing to follow Shara.

As the cliff wall came into view, tension drained from Norrin's shoulders. Shara's wings spread wide, using the wind to push them toward the gray barrier. Banners streamed from every building beyond, symbolizing Ortica's reasserted openness. Birds flocked through the sky over most nations, but in Ortica, a rainbow of dragons patrolled their territory.

Four dragons swooped toward Shara, all bearing banners of white laced with blue. Norrin steered toward them, ready to make his presence known. Before calling out, he raised his hands in greeting. "My name is Norrin. I have come to answer the Prince of Ortica."

One of the approaching riders laughed. "We don't have time for gags, kid."

Norrin shook his head. "The wind passage I just left was guarded by Laktus and Sag-an."

All the riders laughed at Norrin.

"Let me pass," Norrin said. "I have the Shard of Night."

The laughing puttered out.

"Come with us," the rider said. "If you're lying, you'll be crowned Queen of the Dungeons." Another rider waved a pair of colored flags, one of them clean and trimmed with reflective gold.

Turning to follow the quartet, Norrin scowled at the rider's statement. Surely the Prince would outlaw such things.

On the ground, Norrin dismounted, breathing deep as his feet settled on the firm surface. Each step pushed back with an unfamiliar level of resistance.

The other riders dismounted, drawing pikes from their saddles. "This way."

Norrin held up a hand. "One moment." He stepped lightly toward Shara's curled neck. At the dragon's head, Norrin patted her soft cheek, careful not to touch either eye on Shara's side. "Keep an eye out for me."

Shara grunted.

The riders led Norrin to a mantorse-drawn carriage. An opulent-robed man stepped out, waving a gold scepter. "Make way, make way."

When everyone stopped, Norrin glanced at the pikes around him. None aimed at him, but he tensed in their presence all the same. The opulent-robed man approached one of the riders. "Why do riders call for the royal archivist?"

Before the riders could speak, Norrin said, "The Prince of Ortica issued a challenge. If someone could bring him the Shard of Night, that person would win his hand in marriage."

The archivist chuckled. "A childish proclamation."

Norrin pulled the token from his pocket. He unfolded a gray cloth that darkened as it fell loose from the bundle. In the heart of the mass, a clear shard glimmered in the sunlight. The shard flared brighter with every passing moment of exposure.

All four riders recoiled from the intense glow. The archivist lunged forward, wrapping the cloth around the shard once more. After staring at Norrin's hands, the opulent-robed man looked up. "We must find you proper robes so you can be announced at once."

"Skip the pleasantries," Norrin said. "Lead me to the Prince. He'll be glad to see me."

The palace towered as high as it stretched out. Cavernous archways and distant ceilings allowed young dragons space to play without disrupting proceedings on the floor. Norrin had been told about the palace when he was young. The words gave him nothing compared to what his eyes drank in.

Several court officials sniffed and grunted as the archivist escorted Norrin past them. "Make way," the archivist always said. "Make way."

Norrin intentionally dusted off his jacket every few steps. It would do the officials good to smell the rest of the world again.

In the heart of the largest chamber, a polished stone throne stretched halfway to the highest ceiling of the palace. Sitting on the dais, a young man with curly brown hair sat up. "What's happening?"

The archivist extended his arms and bowed before the throne. "Your Highness, forgive the abrupt entrance, but your challenge has been answered."

Gasps and murmurs echoed through the chamber. The Prince stood, brushing a curl from his forehead. "Are you sure? Others have claimed success before."

Norrin stepped in front of the archivist and bowed. "Yes, Prince Marlem. I promised to bring you the Shard of Night when we were young."

"You promised?" The Prince's brow lifted and he stepped to the edge of the dais. His skin paled before he spoke. "Only one person ever promised me to find the Shard."

Standing, Norrin smiled. "An impossible relic from the farthest point in the world." Norrin extended the bundle of cloth to the Prince. "I'm sorry it took so long to find it."

One of the officials spoke. "Lies. The rider is trying to take what we have worked so hard to restore."

"Reject him, Highness."

More of the officials yelled, objecting enough to drown each other out. Norrin sank in the sea of noise, while a row of guards filed around the dais.

One voice bellowed out, silencing the crowd. "You will not reject him."

Muted, the officials backed away from the passage leading into the chamber. A man in onyx armor used a pike as a cane and hobbled toward the throne. "You have not forgotten me," Laktus said. He pulled off his helmet and slipped to one knee. The pike clattered on the floor.

"Noble Laktus. You swore not to return without the Shard of Night." The Prince closed his arms around his chest. "I never thought you were a liar."

"I have broken my vow, but I must speak for this man's bravery." Laktus looked up at Norrin and nodded. "I refused to let him pass, but justice and cunning cast me aside. If anyone is worthy of you, Highness, it is this rider."

The Prince touched one guard's shoulder, making an opening. "Norrin of Tensei." A strained smile grew over the Prince's face. "Am I dreaming?"

Norrin unfolded the cloth again. The Shard's luster filled the chamber. Many officials gasped, but none uttered a single word.

"If you are dreaming," Norrin said, "then I finally caught up with you."

The Prince rushed forward, pressing his lips into Norrin's. All title and pretense set aside, for only a moment.

The archivist cried out. "A suitor worthy of our Prince." The officials repeated the line, but Norrin didn't care. It only mattered that he could taste Marlem's lips once more.

AFTERWARD

This book is a major experiment for me.

First of all, this is my first full release after socially transitioning from Len Berry to Alyssa Askani. Seems fitting since much of what drives life in The Night Lands is the continued drive to change. Such is life and all its survival pressures.

Second, this is the first time I've assembled my short fiction. For a while, I used my Patreon as a way to write new tales. That's why I have so much gathered in these pages.

In no way is this an exhaustive telling of life in this bizarre setting. I've devoted hundreds of thousands of words to the likes of Atsuko Vanity, to the occupied city of Mono, to a rich culture deep under the earth.

Why haven't I unleashed those stories upon the world?

Honestly, I wasn't sure if I was capable of doing them justice before. I feel more capable to pulling off that feat now.

I called this my most brutal setting. There were points in 2019 where I wanted to write more, but I couldn't. I keep confronting the things Sorcha Kagatsu does and decided it was too much for me. She's one of the most defining characters in this world; by now, you've seen what she's capable.

Years ago, I was taking part in a villainous fantasy anthology, *The Rogue's Gallery*. I asked the publisher, Michael Ignacio, Jr., one defining question. "If my story is a movie, what rating can it be?""R, I guess."

"Remember you said that."He didn't. Danny Wilkens, the editor did, but Michael didn't. Not at first.

I turned in "The Mirror of Tila" months later. Michael was concerned. He worried that I'd been abused as a child or experienced some horrific trauma. After all, I'd earned that R rating on the first page.

I assure you, I did not have a traumatic childhood.

What I have is a devotion to presenting my characters to the full extent of what they can do. If I'm writing a villain story, then that villain needs to be suitably horrific in their actions.

When *The Rogue's Gallery* released, "The Mirror of Tila" was the lead story. I didn't want to scare people that severely with this book, so I took a different first step. You have to give some stakes before unleashing full force of creativity or brutality on an audience.

Sometimes we have to unleash the worst dreams upon the page to create the finest heroism. That's my intent with "Mighty Wings," that and I felt like I had to write a dragon battle somewhere along the way.

With enough battles and dragons immersed in this setting, I knew I had to offer that. I wanted a beacon of hope. In time, all monsters can be conquered.

This is a world where I wove together the most video game elements. My dragons are directly inspired by *Panzer Dragoon Orta*. The concept of a world always looking directly up at the sun came from *Shin Megami Tensei: Nocturne* long before I saw the opening credits for *Game of Thrones*.

The reanimated knight Carson was my first *Dark Souls* character. His charge Lora is an idealized take on pyromancers in the first game with some fighting skills from *Dark Souls II*.

There are so many ceramic weapons because of *Nausicaa of the Valley of the Wind*.

If there is a repository for wild influences, it has collided here in its most raw, brutal form. Perhaps my muse has collided with your imagination enough to conjure a few dreams.

Many thanks to you for inviting me to inspire such notions.

No creative effort exists in a vacuum. Without readers, those who write simply languish in solitude. I'd appreciate a review, or a kind word, or a recommendation of my work to a friend.

Community makes us all stronger.

ALSO BY THE AUTHOR

Vitamin F
Scars of Shadow
Loyalty of Severus

Please join me online

Website | https://len-berry.com/
Linktree | https://linktr.ee/lenberry
Patreon | https://www.patreon.com/LenBerry
Ko-Fi | https://ko-fi.com/alyssaaskaniwriting

About the Author

Alyssa Askani is a badass, inspirational writing queen. Don't let her Amazonian size and strength fool you—her mind burns with the fire of a thousand suns while her heart beats with the thunder of a million gods. As an editor and author specializing in science fiction and dark fantasy, Alyssa channels dreamlike storytelling and emotional drives to help writers craft immersive, engaging worlds. Passionate about compelling prose and dynamic narratives, she also writes as Len Berry, Writer of Ethereal Darkness. In either guise, Alyssa is always empowering others to tell their best stories.